MW01134603

LOVE'S STRATEGY

SAMANTHA KANE

SK PUBLISHING LLC

Love's Strategy

Brothers in Arms, Book Three.

Valentine Westridge and Kurt Schillig are lovers, and have been since the Peninsular War when lonely young officer Valentine let himself be seduced by the equally lonely Kurt. Now they're back from the war and intent on beginning the future they dreamed of together, one that includes a quiet country estate, horses, dogs, children, and each other. Their plan, however, also requires a wife. At the suggestion of a mutual friend, Valentine and Kurt believe the financial security they can offer to impoverished widow Leah Marleston will help her accept the unusual sexual relationship they are suggesting.

Leah is at her wit's end, creditors having taken everything she owns to pay off her late husband's gambling debts. She must find a way to support herself and her two children, or be forced to marry her abusive and obsessive brother-in-law. In Valentine's and Kurt's arms, Leah discovers a passion she never knew existed. Brought together by necessity, bonded by desire, these three lonely people find themselves fighting against all odds for a love that was never part of their plans.

ALL RIGHTS RESERVED

Love's Strategy Copyright © 2007 Samantha Kane

Warning: The unauthorized reproduction or distribution of this copyrighted work is illegal. No part of this book may be scanned, uploaded or distributed via the Internet or any other means, electronic or print, without the publisher's permission. Criminal copyright infringement, including infringement without monetary gain, is investigated by the FBI and is punishable by up to 5 years in federal prison and a fine of $250,000. (http://www.fbi.gov/ipr/).

This book is a work of fiction and any resemblance to persons living or dead, or places, events or locales is purely coincidental. The characters are products of the author's imagination and used fictitiously.

❀ Created with Vellum

ACKNOWLEDGMENTS

Thanks go to all the RWA authors and organizations that helped me with Regency research. Any errors contained herein, alas, are the sole responsibility of the author.

This book, like all that have come before, could not have been written without the support of family and friends. So...

...for Will, who wishes to be known from here on out as my Smokin' Hot Big Brother (SHBB), for being a font of historical and literary knowledge, and for his interest in all aspects of writing. And of course his SHW, Kathy (sorry, ladies);

...for my sister Jeri, who finally bought an e-book reader; and

...for my ever-lovin', who cooks, cleans, does the laundry and watches the hooligans so I can live the dream. He read this book approximately five hundred times, and only complained the last hundred. For that, rest assured, dear reader, he received more than a heartfelt thanks.

CHAPTER 1

"*L*eah, there are two gentlemen here to see you."

Leah's blood ran cold at her mother's announcement. More? Were they never to leave her alone? She slowly straightened from where she was bent over tending the roses. February had been decidedly warm this year. She put a hand to the small of her back, realizing even as she did it that it wasn't her back that was really bothering her. She was just so tired. Tired of the incessant demands of creditors, and tired of trying to make ends meet as those same creditors relieved them of everything of value.

"Mama?" Her son Sebastian also stood up where he'd been playing soldiers with his younger sister Esme. Leah's heart contracted at the concern on his face. Ten was too young to carry such worry. She made a deliberate effort to lighten her features as she smiled at him.

"It's nothing, Bastian, just my poor old back aching," she told him lightly, making a face. "You wait here with Esme while I go see what these gentlemen want."

Her mother walked across the garden to join her. At Leah's comment she put a comforting hand on her daughter's arm. "They

1

are not here about one of Thomas' debts, Leah," she said gently, and Leah's eyes inexplicably filled with tears.

"How do you know?" Leah was alarmed at the tremor in her voice. She had held herself together this long, now was not the time to fall apart. Although really, she thought irreverently, when was a good time to fall apart?

Her mother got a very self-righteous look on her face, almost militant. "I asked."

Leah gasped in horror. "You what?"

"I asked them," her mother repeated, her expression mulish. "I'll not have you bothered anymore by those rude upstarts strutting through here demanding their ill-gotten gains."

Leah closed her eyes in despair. "Mother, they have every right. All those debts were legitimately incurred by Thomas before his death."

"Gambling is hardly legitimate—" her mother began, but Leah cut her off.

"They are legally binding debts according to the laws of England, Mother, and as his widow I am legally bound to make restitution."

Marjorie must have recognized the soul-deep exhaustion in Leah's voice because for once she let the subject of Leah's late husband drop. "My dear, let me get rid of these gentlemen. You go upstairs and rest and I'll watch the children for a while."

Leah smiled at her mother. She could be a trial, but under it all Leah knew she loved her unconditionally. "No, Mother, it's best I find out what they want. You stay here with the children, and I shall return as soon as possible." She started to walk away backward, wagging a finger playfully at her mother. "And no more asking strange gentlemen if they are here to collect money, understood?"

~

*V*alentine stood next to the empty hearth, trying not to brood. He'd never even seen the widow, for God's sake, and here he was about to ask for her hand in marriage. It was insane, and it was demoralizing that he and Kurt had to resort to taking advantage of a woman in desperate straits in order to have the life they wished for.

He looked over at Kurt. Kurt glanced up and, quirking an eyebrow, curved one corner of his lips in an amused smile. "Try not to brood, Valentine," he admonished, his German accent subtly lending a continental flavor to his upper-class British tones. He unfurled his long, lean frame from the small parlor chair in which he had been resting. "You'll scare away the poor Widow Marleybone with that expression."

"I am not brooding. And it's Marleston," Valentine corrected with exasperation, "Widow Marleston. For God's sake, if you're going to make me marry her, at least get her name right."

Kurt shrugged. "She won't have it for long, so it's a moot point."

Valentine growled in frustration. "You don't know she'll say yes."

Kurt looked at Valentine incredulously. "Surely you jest? Based on what her mother said, she's in sore need of a hero right now."

"I do not in any way resemble anyone's hero." Valentine rolled his eyes at Kurt's exaggeration. "To the widow I'll more likely resemble a villain, here to take advantage of her straitened circumstances."

Kurt let his gaze wander slowly up and down Valentine's tall, muscular frame, and Valentine felt his cheeks heat at the other man's perusal. He looked guiltily at the door, hoping the Widow Marleston didn't appear while Kurt was devouring him with his eyes.

Kurt laughed at Valentine's look. "Sooner, rather than later, the sweet widow will figure out we're lovers, Valentine. I think it's best done right away, considering I want to be her lover as well." Before Valentine could answer Kurt continued. "As for what you look like," he paused, his eyes moving over Valentine again, "you are very desirable, hero or villain."

"Kurt," was all he said in an admonishing tone. Kurt merely shrugged expansively, in that purely continental way.

Valentine sat in one of the damned uncomfortable chairs that filled the parlor. He slumped forward and ran his hand through his hair. "I don't know whether I feel like the villain or the victim, Kurt."

"Darling Valentine, even Stephen agrees. She is English, and you have a much more respectable English background than I. She will feel more comfortable marrying you. It is a simple thing really, and meaningless in the long run. She will be wife to us both."

Valentine looked up at Kurt. "And if she says no?"

Kurt shrugged expansively again. "Then there are surely other poor widows in England who are desperate."

Valentine laughed. "Desperate enough to take on the two of us? I'm not so sure."

Kurt smiled wickedly. "Ah, *liebchen*, you underestimate my powers of persuasion."

CHAPTER 2

*W*hen Leah stepped into the parlor the two men inside rose from their chairs and turned to her. They were so handsome—tall, lean, muscular, and dressed very expensively. One was dark, his hair a deep brown and his skin an olive tone. The other was quite fair with blond hair and a creamy complexion. Leah had never known men such as these—wealthy and clearly privileged. She was minor country gentry, as Thomas had been.

The dark one stepped forward. "Mrs. Marleston?"

"Yes," Leah answered, wincing at the distrust in her voice that was second nature to her now.

"I am Mr. Valentine Westridge and this is Mr. Kurt Schillig," he said, indicating the tall blond with a sweep of his hand.

"How do you do," Leah said politely, never moving from the open door. "How may I help you?"

The two men exchanged a look that Leah found hard to interpret. Mr. Westridge spoke once again. "Perhaps this letter will help," and he pulled something from his pocket. Leah looked at it with distaste. All her late husband's creditors appeared with "letters".

She sighed. "I'm sorry, gentlemen, I really haven't anything left to pay you. All my worldly goods have been sold to pay previous debts I'm afraid. This house is not mine nor are any of its furnishings. You may choose to pursue this debt in the courts, but other than finding myself in debtors' prison, I'm quite sure that very little will come of it."

The dark, enigmatic Mr. Westridge turned red, with embarrassment, Leah wondered? Then the beautiful blond Mr. Schillig stepped forward. How delightful, Leah thought irrelevantly, that this bad news was delivered by such gorgeous specimens of manhood.

Mr. Schillig took the letter from Mr. Westridge's hand and walked over to Leah. She automatically extended her hand to receive it, and he placed it there gently.

"You misunderstand, Mrs...my dear," he said quietly. His accent was quite lovely, actually. "This is a letter of introduction from a mutual friend, Mr. Stephen Matthews."

Leah was very confused now. "The Reverend Mr. Matthews?" she asked. Mr. Schillig nodded with a small smile. Leah was shocked to feel herself responding to that smile, responding to him as a man. She had felt dead, that way, for years now, since long before Thomas's death.

She took the note and began to read.

Valentine was eternally grateful that Kurt had taken over because Valentine was struck nearly speechless by the poor Widow Marleston. She was, well, perfect. The top of her perfect head reached Kurt's shoulder. That would put her just a little taller next to him. Her hair was a glorious shade of red gold, upswept to reveal a long, graceful neck and creamy soft skin. His mouth watered with the desire to taste that neck, just there where her pulse beat so swiftly. She was very curvaceous. It was obvious she was used to carrying more weight, however. Clearly her circumstances had taken their toll in more ways than the dark circles under her eyes.

The suspicion in her voice and matter-of-fact recitation of her desperate financial situation nearly made him act the fool. He was willing to do anything for her, to protect her, to possess her. He'd almost blurted that out, hardly the sophisticated approach he'd been practicing. Why hadn't Stephen prepared them? Passably pretty, he'd said with a sly grin. Valentine had taken that to mean barely tolerable. He knew now it had been Stephen's idea of a joke.

Valentine took several slow steps back, mentally and physically. He needed that distance to get his thoughts back in order. He came to rest in his earlier position, next to the hearth. The empty hearth now represented times the lovely widow had done without, had gone cold or hungry because she couldn't afford the basic necessities for herself and her children. Never again, he vowed. She and hers would never want for anything ever again. He looked away from the dark, cold fireplace and directly into the widow's eyes.

Kurt's heart was racing. This was not what he had planned at all, not at all. He'd planned on Valentine making a pleasant connection with a woman whom he married for the purpose of having children, and who married him for financial security. A woman they would share when the mood struck but who remained a firm outsider in relation to his and Valentine's close attachment. Instead, Valentine was stricken with love at the first sight of the lovely widow. Kurt himself felt something stirring in his chest, in the place he thought was so full of Valentine no other could find room there. She was beautiful, obviously courageous, and she possessed a certain dignity and self-assurance. She was a woman with few equals. The kind of woman a man like Valentine searched his whole life for and, once found, lived his whole life for. Kurt had trouble breathing as he tried to imagine what would happen to him if Valentine were to turn him away, if the lovely Mrs. Marleston refused Valentine's initial offer, refused Kurt.

He and Valentine had been together since one fateful night during the war, when Kurt was so desperately lonely and could no longer resist the temptation of the lovely young British officer whom he'd befriended. And Valentine, equally lonely, equally desperate, had let himself be seduced by the sophisticated half-German officer. They had found in one another the tenderness and passion that the war leached out of them, filling the empty spaces that the violence and bloodshed left behind. After the war it was only natural that they stayed together. Kurt couldn't even imagine life without Valentine.

Now he had argued and coerced Valentine into doing the one thing that might tear them apart. He'd forced him to fall in love with a woman and marry. He'd thought to give Valentine the one thing missing in their lives, children and the respectability of a wife. Valentine longed for the quiet life of a country squire and Kurt was more than happy to share that life and that dream. Valentine insisted he didn't need a wife and family to make him happy, that he was happy with Kurt. But Kurt knew Valentine better than he knew himself and he had set out to give him what he needed, just as he had endeavored to give Valentine everything he needed or wanted since their first night together. Old habits die hard, Kurt thought wryly as he watched Valentine watch the widow.

Kurt turned his attention to Mrs. Marleston and he felt his cock stir. If only she would say yes the three of them together would be glorious. Not just for one night, but every night for the rest of their lives. Kurt's eyes widened in shock. Perhaps this wasn't just Valentine's dream, but his as well. A dream that had taken root, he thought, when they'd heard their old friends Jason Randall and Tony Richards had taken a wife. According to Stephen, the ceremony had included all three, with Stephen presiding, and now the three were expecting a child. If they could have it all, why not Kurt and Valentine? Kurt took a deep breath, firming his resolve. Yes, indeed, why not?

When Leah's eyes met Mr. Westridge's she was shocked by the intensity of his gaze. Stephen Matthews' letter had simply said that he'd known both Mr. Westridge and Mr. Schillig during the war on the Peninsula, and they were both trustworthy gentlemen. He urged her to listen to them with an open mind and an open heart. That was all. He gave no indication of what they wanted from her. She had befriended the young and handsome vicar upon her arrival in Ashton on the Green, and she trusted his judgment. If he said she should listen to his friends, then she would. But what could they possibly want?

"All right, I've read Mr. Matthews' letter, and I'm more than willing to listen to whatever you have to say. But I'm rather confused. Pardon my directness, but what could two gentlemen such as you require from me?" She glanced at the two men and intercepted yet another cryptic look between them. Her suspicions grew when they both hesitated to speak.

Suddenly Mr. Westridge stepped forward again, as if to speak. Leah gave him an encouraging smile, but the words seemed to die in his throat. Slightly exasperated, she turned to Mr. Schillig.

He cleared his throat with a gentle cough before speaking. "We are, um, aware of your circumstances, Mrs. Marleston, and we are here to offer you an advantageous proposition."

Leah felt the blood drain from her face as her back went stiff. "I am not so desperate as to accept that kind of offer, Mr. Schillig. Good day." She turned to the door, furious with Mr. Matthews and these so-called gentlemen.

"Oh that was marvelous, Kurt. This is surely a more disastrous misunderstanding than the one I caused." Mr. Westridge's voice was agitated, but underlying it was amusement, and Leah whirled around to give him the dressing-down he deserved. Before she could speak Mr. Westridge held up his hands as if to ward her off.

9

"No, no, truly you misunderstood. I, we, are not offering you… you *carte blanche*, Mrs. Marleston. Far from it. You can't think Stephen would condone that, do you?"

Leah was stopped short by his behavior and his words. No, she would not like to think the kind vicar would condone that, but she'd been dealt some harsh blows of reality in the last few years.

"Well, it is *carte blanche* of a sort, Valentine," Mr. Schillig said, "of your very generous fortune, and mine as well."

Leah found her gaze divided between them again as she tried to decipher that statement. She was having a hard time deciding whether to be angry or merely confused.

"Would you give me the courtesy, Kurt, of letting me negotiate my own marriage contract?" Mr. Westridge said tightly.

Leah's reply was arrested by that one word—marriage. She took two small steps back into the room. "You had best explain yourselves better than this. I will grant you but a few more minutes to make your business plain, or I will be forced to ask you to leave."

Mr. Westridge took a step closer, and Leah could see the determination on his face. "We are here to offer you marriage, Mrs. Marleston."

Leah was dumfounded. "Both of you? You are here to court me?"

"No, we are here to ask you to marry us," Mr. Westridge said earnestly.

Leah could not control the incredulity of her expression. "Did Mr. Matthews put you up to this? Is one of you to be the sacrificial lamb? I told him I would not marry him just to solve my financial difficulties. The same applies to any of his friends."

"Not one of us, Mrs. Marleston," Mr. Schillig said smoothly, "both of us."

"No, not both of us," Mr. Westridge seemed to be stammering. "I mean yes, both of us, but you will be my wife. And not lambs.

Not sacrificial lambs. You see, we want to marry you. We need to marry you."

Leah's mind was reeling. "You both need to marry me? That's impossible. What on earth do you mean?"

Mr. Westridge sighed in frustration as he ran a hand through his dark hair, leaving unruly curls behind. "This is not going according to my plan at all."

CHAPTER 3

*J*ust then Mrs. Marleston's mother and children came through the door.

"Oh I'm sorry!" Mrs. Northcott cried. "I didn't realize you were still with your guests, Leah."

Leah. Her name was Leah, Valentine thought. It was lovely and suited the woman perfectly. He looked down at the children and suddenly realized if all went as he hoped they would be his children. The boy looked to be about nine or ten, a sturdy lad with a shock of red hair and blue eyes as suspicious as his mother's. The little girl couldn't be above five, with golden curls and blue eyes that nearly filled her face. He fell in love on the spot.

"Hello," Valentine said, bending his knees so he could look them in the eye. "I'm Mr. Westridge."

"Good afternoon, sir," the boy said stiffly. The little girl moved behind her brother and stuck her thumb in her mouth as she peeked out around his legs.

Valentine suppressed a smile. "And what are your names?"

The boy looked up at Leah, and she nodded. "I am Sebastian, and my sister is Esme." Then he looked pointedly at Kurt.

Kurt laughed, and Valentine watched everyone relax. Kurt's

laugh often had that effect. It was low and deep and jolly. "I am Mr. Schillig. Do you speak German?"

The boy shook his head, and the little girl quickly pulled her head back behind his legs like a little turtle.

"Well, you shall soon." Kurt looked at Leah as he said it, and she frowned back at him.

"Are you a new tutor then?" Sebastian asked eagerly.

Leah stepped forward at that point and put her hand on Sebastian's shoulder. "No, dear, Mr. Schillig is a just a nice friend of Mr. Matthews. You know we can't afford a tutor right now." The crestfallen look on the boy's face endeared him even more to Valentine. How he would enjoy a son who loved learning.

"Mother, why don't you and the children have tea and then you can supervise Bastian's studies while this little one," she tapped a finger on Esme's not so hidden nose, "takes a nap." She turned to look at her mother. "I shall be in the garden with Mr. Westridge and Mr. Schillig."

"Is everything all right, dear?" Mrs. Northcott asked.

"Yes, Mother, everything is fine. These two gentlemen are friends of Mr. Matthews. He sent a letter of introduction with them."

"Oh, well, that's nice."

Mrs. Northcott was clearly confused, but Leah did not enlighten her. Instead she turned to Valentine and Kurt. "Shall we, gentlemen?" She indicated the door, and Kurt gestured that she should precede them. Mrs. Northcott and the children moved out of their way. Valentine saw Kurt give little Esme a broad smile as he left, and the tiny tot popped her thumb out of her mouth to return it.

~

*O*nce in the garden, Valentine made several attempts to begin the conversation. Kurt tried to let him lead in this, but despite his usual disarming charm Valentine seemed to stumble over the words.

"You see, Mrs. Marleston," Valentine began, "sometimes in war, well, men you see," he paused and coughed, "that is to say, companions can often become, um…close, you see."

Leah looked at him in confusion. "Well, of course men are drawn closer by their shared experiences, Mr. Westridge."

"Yes, yes, exactly," Valentine said happily. "And Kurt and I are, er, were, brought closer by the war."

"So you were there with Mr. Matthews?" Leah asked helpfully.

"Yes, quite right, we were." Valentine was less sure of himself here. It was obvious Leah had no idea what he was talking about.

Valentine heaved a giant sigh. "Mrs. Marleston," he began again, stopping in the path beside a small rustic bench, "Kurt and I both wish to marry you because of our relationship."

Leah and Kurt had stopped as well, and Leah looked back and forth between the men. "Because you are friends, you both wish to marry me?"

"Exactly," Valentine said, nodding his head decisively.

As Leah and Valentine stared at one another uncomprehendingly, Kurt rolled his eyes and shook his head. He stepped forward until he was next to the two of them, the three forming a loose triangle on the path.

"May I?" he asked Valentine politely.

"Oh, oh yes, please do," Valentine said, and he began to step back. Kurt stopped him with a hand on his arm.

Kurt turned to Leah, who smiled at him encouragingly. She was really quite breathtakingly lovely, Kurt thought, smiling back. And she was so sweet to poor tongue-tied Valentine.

"We," Kurt began, waving a hand between himself and Valentine, "are lovers and have been since the war. We wish to take a wife—a woman who will be wife to both of us, in and out of the bedroom. We wish to have a family. We want to have all this with you and still remain lovers."

~

*T*he sound that escaped Leah's throat at the blunt declaration could best be described as a squeak. She stumbled back a step, suddenly lightheaded.

"Mrs. Marleston!" cried Mr. Westridge as he rushed forward to grab her arm. "Let me help you," he implored, guiding her gently to the bench directly behind her. When her knees hit the bench she sat with an undignified thump.

Mr. Schillig came up next to him with a look of concern. "I can see that I've alarmed you, and that was not my intention. I apologize."

"No, no," she said, and her voice sounded weak. She cleared her throat. "I mean, I'm...startled. This is hardly something I'm familiar with. I've heard stories, of course, but I've never met anyone who...that is...does Mr. Matthews know?"

Her face felt pale and she found it hard to look at Mr. Schillig. Mr. Westridge sat down next to her on the bench, and she thought it showed remarkable restraint that she didn't immediately throw herself off in an attempt to get away from him. These were such intimate subjects; she'd never had such a conversation before.

"Yes, Stephen knows," Mr. Westridge answered her. "He was the one who suggested we seek you out when we told him what we were planning. He said you were a sensible woman who would see the advantages in the situation."

"What advantages?" Leah asked, still reeling in shock. Mr. Matthews knew, and he apparently approved!

"You are in desperate financial straits, Leah," Mr. Westridge said gently. She knew she should chastise him for using her Christian name, but it sounded so wonderful when he said it. "I can help, we can help. We are both wealthy men. We can pay your debts, take care of you and the children properly. We can give you a fine home, and clothes, plentiful food, fires in the winter and a name to go with them—my name."

"Mr. Schillig—" she began, but he cut her off.

"Kurt, I am Kurt," he said softly, smiling at her. Her stomach flip-flopped at the thought of using his given name. Then Mr. Westridge picked up her hand and slid closer on the bench.

"And I am Valentine," he said, kissing her hand. She felt the kiss deep in her core, and the fire there surprised her. She couldn't possibly be considering this, could she?

She looked back at the tall blond man before her. What she had to ask wasn't the most pertinent question, considering all they had just told her, but it was the one uppermost in her mind. "Kurt," she tried out, speaking his name slowly. She was rewarded with another smile. "What do you hope to gain if I am to take Mr. Westridge's name?" At the slight squeeze of her hand she looked over. "Valentine, I mean Valentine." He also rewarded her with a smile.

"I will gain the same thing as Valentine, my dear, a wife and a mother for my children."

Leah's stomach clenched at his words. No, not her stomach, lower, and it was desire that caused it, not disgust. Her eyes widened as she stared at him, and she saw his brown eyes deepen with an answering desire as if he knew what she was feeling.

"This is something you would gain from also?" he asked, his accent more pronounced than it had been before.

"Perhaps," Leah said slowly. She licked her lips nervously, her agitation growing when she saw Mr. Schillig, no Kurt, watching her mouth avidly. "But you must understand this is quite shocking to me. May I...may I inquire as to why you wish to take a wife?"

"Of course, Leah. I'm sure you have a great many questions." Valentine sighed. "I know this is highly unusual—" Leah couldn't stop her snort of disbelief at the sheer magnitude of that understatement. Valentine merely arched a brow and continued, "But we hope you will at least consider our proposal." He rubbed a thumb over her knuckles, and Leah was startled to realize he still held her hand. She gently disengaged it and folded both hands in her lap. Valentine smiled a little wistfully and moved away from her slightly, clearly recognizing her need for more space. If she was to seriously consider their proposal she needed her mind unclouded by the nearness of him.

Leah waited patiently for him to answer her question. Valentine leaned forward and placed his elbows on his knees, staring at the ground between his feet. "I mentioned earlier that Kurt and I were on the Peninsula together." He looked over at Leah and she nodded.

"Yes, with Mr. Matthews."

"Yes, with Stephen and so many others. Do you know much of war, Leah?" The question was asked casually but Leah noticed Valentine's hands were fisted.

"No, Valentine," she said softly, "not about the most recent I'm afraid. My own personal struggles took precedence over the news sheets."

Valentine looked away and nodded. "That's as it should be." He sat back on the bench and looked at Kurt. "So many times we wondered, why are we here? What are we fighting for? What are our friends dying for? As young men you think it's glory, heroism. But if you are there long enough you realize it's more important things. Things such as honor and tradition, a way of life. You begin to categorize what's important to you." He looked at Leah. "Do you understand?"

Did she understand prioritizing your life? Oh yes, she understood. She'd had to do that many times over in the last few years. What was more important, the financial security of marrying an abusive bully, or shielding her children from the abuse they might suffer? And after that decision, what was more important, having new clothes to maintain a veneer of respectability and perhaps catch the eye of a potential husband, or making sure her children ate well? And on down the line, each decision altering her future until this moment. And now yet another decision stood before her. As with all her past decisions she would try to make a well-informed choice, but it would always, as in everything she did, be what was best for her children. They were the most important thing to her, their welfare her main concern. Valentine tipped his head to the side and regarded her quizzically and she realized she had not answered his question. "Yes, I understand having to choose what is most important to you."

Kurt spoke from where he had moved to lean against a tree a few feet from the bench. "Not so much choose as decide. I do not believe we were in the same situation as you, Leah."

Leah blushed as she saw the sympathetic look in his eyes. "No, Mr. Schillig. In my experience, men rarely are." Kurt merely nodded once in acceptance of this fact. Still looking at Kurt, Leah asked, "And what was important to you?"

"Valentine," was Kurt's simple reply.

Leah turned to Valentine, who was smiling wryly. "He over-simplifies. We were important to one another, the most important thing, to be accurate. But we did not just want to survive. For many who were there too long survival became the main goal. But I, we, wanted more. We wanted a future."

"Yes," Kurt whispered, and when Leah looked Kurt had turned away to stare off into the hills in the distance.

"We thought very hard about what kind of future we could have, and what kind of future we wanted. As you can imagine in our situation the two are not always the same." Valentine's voice held a bitter note.

"That is true in most cases, Valentine, not just for you and Kurt." Leah's tone was bitter as well. How well she knew the taste of future happiness turned to ashes in the ruin of what was, never to experience what could have been.

"Of course. I guess we tend to forget everyone else's troubles in light of our own. I'm sorry, Leah."

Leah smiled wryly. "Yes, well, I've been rather wrapped up in my own troubles as well. Please, go on."

Valentine sighed. "There's not much more actually. What I wanted was a simple life. I wanted a nice country life, a modest home, a pretty wife, children. I want my most pressing concern to be whether it is hunting season or racing season. I want a pack of dogs, a houseful of children, and with all that I want Kurt."

"And Kurt?" Leah asked, watching the blond man slowly turn to look at her.

"I have already told you. I want Valentine."

"I see." And truly she did. They were obviously in love with one another, a concept that should have shocked her but didn't. She understood that when your back was to the wall you could no longer lie to yourself. You found yourself doing or saying things you never would have before, but when you had nothing left to lose what did it matter? When these two men were faced with death on a daily basis they looked at one another and with perfect clarity realized this is what I want, this is what I'm fighting for. And they survived. Leah had survived for her children.

"Why me?" Leah's question wasn't vanity. While she knew she was attractive, she had almost nothing else to recommend her to a potential mate. She was worse than penniless since she had unpaid debts, she had two young children, and no familial connections. "Surely there were women in London, women with whom you were acquainted, that you could have asked?"

Kurt straightened from the tree. "We did. They would not have us."

"Oh I beg your pardon," Leah said, startled and a little embarrassed. "I just assumed I was the first woman you had approached." She smiled self-deprecatingly. "But now I understand, I am a last resort, am I not?"

Valentine looked very embarrassed but Kurt eyed her with

approval. "You understand then where we are coming from, yes?" Kurt asked shrewdly.

"Why would they not have you?" Leah wanted to know if there was more objectionable about the two gentlemen than the fact that they were lovers. She surprised herself with that thought. Already, knowing them for less than an hour, the thought of their being lovers was unexceptional to Leah. Now that she understood them a little at least, she found them to be amiable and honest, so far. Coupled with their expensive attire and their assurances that they were financially able to take care of Leah and the children, these attributes far outweighed their unusual relationship.

Valentine looked uncomfortable. "They naturally objected to our relationship. We first approached a woman I knew before the war. She is now a widow and we'd hoped that being sexually knowledgeable she would understand that our being lovers was not the horrific act so many people decry. Particularly since she knew me before I met Kurt, we thought she would be tolerant. As we mentioned, we are both wealthy men and we thought that in exchange for our wealth she, or someone like her, would accept both of us."

Kurt snorted in disgust. "She swooned with horror and then shrieked for us to get out. She did not wish anyone to know that we thought she would accept such an 'unnatural', to use her word, relationship. Her vitriolic response made us more cautious. We waited months before approaching another woman. Valentine courted her singly, although I saw her and spoke to her numerous times. Only when she had softened toward Valentine and indicated she would be receptive to a proposal did we go to her and explain our situation. She didn't bother to swoon. She slapped Valentine's face and accused me of being a vile seducer of good Englishmen, and threw us out."

"But she would have taken you, Valentine? On your own? I'm sure many women would. Why didn't you pursue that avenue, marrying individually and still keeping Kurt, separate from your marriage?"

Valentine was shaking his head before she even finished speaking. "No, that is not what I want. I want Kurt. Everything else is for us, not just for me." The glance the two men exchanged made Leah catch her breath. Valentine looked back at her and sighed. "After her dismissal I confided in Stephen Matthews." He smiled at Leah. "He said he knew the perfect woman for us. I begin to believe he was right."

Kurt chuckled. "At least you have not been slapped yet."

"So merely on Mr. Matthews' recommendation you traveled all the way from London to ask me to marry you?"

"Oh no, I'm sorry. I haven't made myself clear," Valentine said, sitting up straighter with a frown. "You see, that's why I was talking to Stephen. We have purchased Cantley House, just a few miles from here. Certainly your familiarity with the area will help greatly as we settle in here."

"Cantley?" Leah asked, surprised. "I didn't know." She chewed her lip nervously. "So you will be living here then?"

Valentine smiled to take the sting out of his words. "Yes, that is our plan, to live quietly in the country as I mentioned before. Not only is Stephen Matthews a friend of ours, but the Duke of Ashland is also a friend. Since Ashford Park is just on the other side of the village, Cantley was a very good find for us."

"So my location was paramount in your decision?"

"No." It was Kurt who answered. "Your financial difficulties were. We thought that you would have too much to gain by wedding us to object to our relationship."

Leah was taken aback at his honest answer. It was rather demoralizing that her greatest asset to these handsome, wealthy war heroes was her destitution. Unfortunately they may be right. Leah thought it was time to get down to business. "I should like some particulars about the marriage settlement."

Valentine's smile grew until it lit up his entire face. "Does that mean yes?"

"I would be a fool to agree before I hear the terms."

They settled down to talk money. Leah ruthlessly crushed the sentimental part of herself that longed for romance and courtship. She wasn't a young girl anymore. She had a family to provide for. She would never leave herself open to the kind of poverty she had suffered since her first marriage. She had been young then with no father or male relation of any kind to ensure a proper marriage settlement. She was older and wiser now.

When they were done Leah was stunned. Valentine and Kurt weren't just wealthy. A friend of theirs was a genius at investing and they had a combined income that was an outrageous amount to someone in Leah's situation. They wished to settle a goodly sum on Leah. She would have the interest of that money to spend as she saw fit. They also promised her extra pin money quarterly, and a generous dowry for Esme and school fees for Bastian.

"Will you marry us, Leah?" Valentine asked as she sat there in shock.

"I…" she hesitated, unsure of how to answer him. Would the money make up for the potential ostracism she and the children might bear should Kurt and Valentine's relationship become public knowledge?

"Please, Leah," begged Valentine, "don't decide now. Take some time to think about it, please." He raised her hand and kissed it again, and Leah's eyes were pulled back to him. He kept her hand pressed lightly to his lips as he spoke. "From the first moment I saw you, I knew you were the one. We were meant to be together, Leah. Just give us a chance to prove it."

His words touched her in a way she hadn't been moved since Thomas had courted her. She felt desirable, pretty, young again. And of course, she *was* in desperate financial straits. She looked at Kurt standing there, his eyes again burning with desire. "All right, Valentine," she whispered. "I will give you a chance."

~

"*T*hen you will come for dinner tomorrow evening," Valentine said for the third or fourth time. Leah smiled. The three had walked around the cottage to where the two men had left their horses beneath a large tree. The small Northcott home had no stables or grooms.

She had agreed to think about their proposal and to meet them the following evening with an answer. "Yes, I'll come. We'd heard that someone had purchased Cantley, but I didn't know it was you."

Kurt stood in the sunshine, his blond hair gleaming. "We were friends with the late brother of the Duke of Ashland during the war, and have come to know the new Duke quite well. His companion, Mr. Haversham, is also a close friend. With Stephen here as well, it seemed the ideal place to settle down."

"So you own the estate?" Leah asked, intrigued. If she were to marry Valentine, would they live in Kurt's home? It was all so confusing to her.

"I have an investment in it," Kurt said, still smiling. "Most of my future is invested in Valentine."

Leah blushed as she was reminded of their relationship. Of course Kurt would consider Valentine's home his own. "I'm sorry, I didn't realize..."

Kurt placed his fashionable beaver hat on his head at a rakish angle. "This is all very new to you, my dear. No apologies are necessary."

Valentine drew her attention when he stepped forward. She turned and found a small frown on his face. "Leah, you must understand that Kurt is, and will always be, a major part of my life, and soon, I hope, yours. We will always live together, travel together. Kurt and I are as close as I want you and I to be someday."

Kurt came up behind Leah and raised her hand for a kiss. "As close as we will all be, soon," he said quietly. Valentine moved closer to her and turned the hand Kurt held to place a kiss upon her palm. "Yes, exactly," he whispered, looking into her eyes.

Leah felt overwhelmed by the two strong male bodies. They enclosed her in a cocoon of heat and male spice, and she couldn't stop her mind from picturing the three of them entangled in the sheets of some large bed. Her mind blanked after that, however. Exactly how did three people make love? She had never minded the marriage act with Thomas; it was nice to be close to someone that way. Kurt moved in closer and she felt his breath on her neck as Valentine touched the tip of his tongue to her palm. Good Lord, Thomas had never done that. Leah's lips parted as she found herself having trouble breathing. Her pulse was racing, and she felt hot and heavy and wet between her legs. She thought perhaps making love with Valentine and Kurt would be more than nice.

CHAPTER 4

"*L*eah?" The male voice was harsh and Kurt's back instantly stiffened. He moved directly behind Leah protectively and when she turned toward the voice her nose was very nearly pressed into his chest. She looked up at Kurt in alarm, mixed with a little annoyance, but he merely raised an eyebrow at her and turned to look over his shoulder at the owner of the voice.

"Leah, what is going on?" The man was short and somewhere between forty and fifty. He had a portly stomach bulging out his too tight, garish coat, and the overall effect was almost comical. Kurt was not fooled, however. That voice indicated this was not a man to take lightly.

"Please, Kurt," Leah whispered, "that is my brother-in-law, Sir Horatio Marleston."

Kurt noticed that Valentine had moved to his side and was facing Sir Horatio.

"Remove yourselves from Mrs. Marleston immediately," Sir Horatio said, and it was apparent from his tone he was used to being obeyed. The look of disbelief on his face when neither Kurt nor Valentine moved made Kurt smile coldly. Leah was pushing ineffectively at his chest, and he gripped her upper arms gently to still her.

"May we help you?" Valentine asked politely, and his tone also spoke volumes. It clearly marked Leah as theirs.

"I demand you release Mrs. Marleston immediately," Sir Horatio replied.

"Oh really, gentlemen." Leah's tone was exasperated, and she gave Kurt a shove that had him stumbling back a step in surprise at her strength. "Sir Horatio is my brother-in-law."

The man reached out as if to grab her arm, but stopped at a sound from Valentine somewhere between a growl and a dangerous purr. Kurt stepped back next to Leah's side.

"Sir Horatio, may I present Mr. Valentine Westridge and Mr. Kurt Schillig," Leah said to him, indicating first Valentine and then Kurt with a graceful gesture of her hand.

"How do you do," Kurt said coldly without a smile. Valentine merely nodded once in acknowledgment.

"What is your business with Mrs. Marleston?" Sir Horatio's voice was still demanding, and the unspoken message was that he had the right to ask. Leah apparently thought differently.

"That is not your concern, Sir Horatio," she said almost as coldly as Kurt. "To what do I owe the pleasure of your visit?" It was subtle, but Kurt caught the sarcasm in her voice.

"I wished to call on you," Sir Horatio told her imperiously, "as I do several times a week." He looked pointedly at the hand Kurt had placed possessively on Leah's elbow.

"Thank you," Leah said automatically. "Mr. Westridge and Mr. Schillig were just leaving. You may go in and see the children."

"I have no desire to see the children," Sir Horatio replied unhesitatingly. "They should be in the schoolroom at this time."

Kurt's estimation of Sir Horatio dipped even lower at his quick dismissal of Bastian and Esme.

Leah sighed in exasperation. "You know I cannot afford a tutor right now, Sir Horatio, and Esme is too young. My mother is with

Bastian working on his lessons right now and will not mind the interruption."

"I will wait for you," Sir Horatio said, and Kurt could practically see his feet planting themselves more firmly on the ground. Kurt turned away, dismissing Sir Horatio, and he heard the older man gasp in outrage.

"We shall send the carriage for you tomorrow at, shall we say seven, then?" Kurt asked Leah. He'd deliberately brought up their plans in front of Sir Horatio. The more obvious they made their claim on Leah, the better as far as he was concerned. She was theirs, by God, and he dared any man to question it.

His own possessiveness concerning her was slightly shocking to him. He could understand Valentine's immediate connection to her, he was a man of deeply felt emotions. But Kurt was usually ruled by the physical, not the emotional, except when it came to Valentine. Was he merely reacting to Valentine's desire for Leah? Or to his own newly acknowledged desire for a home and children? Or was it the woman herself? Leah answered his question before Kurt could examine his motives too closely.

"Yes, yes that would be fine," Leah said in a rush, and Kurt saw her cheeks were pink with embarrassment.

"Mrs. Marleston is already engaged for tomorrow evening," Sir Horatio interrupted harshly.

Leah's eyes flew to the older man and narrowed. "I'm sorry, Sir Horatio, but I'm afraid I do not know of a previous engagement."

"That is why I came to see you, my dear," Sir Horatio said with a tight smile. "You did not respond to my note, and I came to make sure that you were going to accompany me to dinner with the Dowager Duchess."

"I received no note," Leah said coldly. "I'm very sorry, but I am promised to dinner at Cantley tomorrow evening."

"Cantley?" Sir Horatio exclaimed, surprised. "Are you the new owner then?" he asked Kurt belligerently. "I had heard the new owner was a war veteran and a close personal friend of the young Duke." His tone indicated disbelief that Kurt could be either.

"I am the new owner of Cantley," Valentine informed him in glacial tones, "although that description does indeed fit Mr. Schillig as well."

"Welcome," Sir Horatio replied, although his tone was anything but. Kurt nearly laughed aloud. It would seem most of this conversation was being conducted in what remained unsaid.

"Sir Horatio's own small estate lies to the east of Cantley, with a portion of the Duke's land in between." Leah supplied the information in a matter-of-fact tone, but Kurt saw Sir Horatio's eyes narrow at her use of the word small. "Next to the Duke, he was the largest landowner in the area until your arrival. There are mainly small holdings here, for the most part."

"I shall have the Dowager Duchess send you an invitation to her dinner tomorrow evening," Sir Horatio told them smoothly. "I'm sure she would have invited you had she known of your arrival in our little society here."

Valentine answered. "As you are aware, we are engaged for tomorrow evening with Mrs. Marleston. Do not trouble yourself on our account."

Kurt grinned broadly at Valentine's blanket dismissal of Sir Horatio's challenge to their plans with Leah.

Sir Horatio turned to look at Leah. "This way Mrs. Marleston will not miss out on dinner at Ashton Park, a supreme privilege, I assure you." Kurt bristled at the man's tenaciousness.

"A privilege I'm sure we shall all enjoy when the Duke is in residence," Valentine smoothly countered, upping the ante in what had become almost a game.

Sir Horatio's smile became even more strained. "The Dowager Duchess would be very unhappy were Leah not to attend tomorrow night. She has taken quite an interest in her future, you know. The Duchess does not believe a young woman like Leah should remain unmarried so long after my brother's death." The unspoken implication was that the Dowager wanted Leah to marry Sir Horatio. Kurt shuddered at the thought.

Leah had clearly had enough and intervened again. She frowned at Sir Horatio. "My married state is not the concern of the Dowager Duchess." She then turned to Kurt and Valentine. "I am so pleased that you came to call today, gentlemen," she assured them firmly, "and I shall see you tomorrow evening."

Valentine looked as if he were about to argue, but Kurt laughed out loud, stopping him. "Yes, my dear Mrs. Marleston, it has indeed been a pleasure." Kurt gave a low courtly bow to her and kissed her hand lingeringly with a twinkle in his eye. Leah laughed in return, which only made Sir Horatio glare harder.

Leah turned to Valentine and held her hand out. He hesitated. "Now, Valentine," Kurt said chidingly and put his arm around Valentine's shoulders companionably. "We are being given our *conge*, my dear. Kiss the lady's hand, and we shall dream together of seeing her again tomorrow night."

Valentine obediently took Leah's hand and sighed. He held her small hand in both of his and raised it to his lips almost reverently. Barely moving away from her hand, he raised his eyes to her face. "I'm sorry, my dear. I did not mean to cause you distress. We shall take our leave. Until tomorrow then."

~

*A*fter Valentine and Kurt rode away, Leah drew a deep breath and turned to Sir Horatio. She was glad she'd had a minute or two to get herself under control after Valentine's goodbye. His eyes had burned so hot when he'd looked at her over her hand she was surprised her hair hadn't gone up in flames. Good heavens, what was wrong with her? She'd never reacted to a gentleman like this before, and today she'd behaved like a wanton with two! And it was impossible to think Sir Horatio had not noticed.

Indeed his visage was nearly purple with rage. "You behaved shamelessly, Leah, and I will not have it." His voice was trembling with his anger. "I will not have my future wife acting the slut with men such as that."

"I am not your future wife." Leah felt her own anger rising. "Men such as what, Sir Horatio? Wealthy, well-mannered, admiring? Which do you find so offensive?"

He was breathing hard he was so angry. "I saw the way the foreigner touched Mr. Westridge. You do not know of such things, Leah, and must be guided by me. They are not the sort of gentlemen who should be calling here at the cottage."

"They had a letter of introduction from Mr. Matthews, and by your own admission are close personal friends with the Duke. I hardly think that puts them beyond the pale, Sir Horatio." She allowed a little of her impatience with his attitude to show in her voice. It was a mistake, and she should have known better. His hand shot out and grabbed her arm, bruising in its grip. She gasped and he tightened his hold. She couldn't help comparing his brutal hold to Kurt's gentle one earlier.

"We have an understanding, my dear. If you wish me to take care of those mewling brats of yours, you will submit to me and be my wife."

Tears came to Leah's eyes as the pressure on her arm became excruciating. She knew from experience that he would leave bruises behind. "We do not have an understanding of any kind," Leah gasped, trying to pry his fingers off her. "You do not have the right to touch me. You have asked for my hand and I have refused you, repeatedly."

"No one else will be offering, Leah, I've made sure they all know you are mine. You have been mine since that fateful day Thomas had to beg my sufferance and moved you all into my house because of his ruin. I do not know why you fight it. Even Thomas accepted it, didn't he?" She could not get his hand off no matter how hard she tried, and he dragged her closer to him until she could feel the press of his erection against her hip as she tried desperately to turn away. "If you cannot take care of those children, I shall petition for guardianship. Do I make myself clear? Do you wish to lose them? Do you wish your mother to lose her home? With one word to the Duchess I can make all of that happen. You will send your regrets to Mr. Westridge and accompany me to Ashton Park tomorrow night, and we will announce our engagement. Do you understand?"

"Leah? Are you all right?" Her mother's voice was slightly tremulous, and Leah looked at her in relief where she stood outside the cottage door. "It is late, Sir Horatio. The children and I are waiting dinner on Leah. I'm sure your business can wait until tomorrow." Mrs. Northcott was frightened of Sir Horatio and his rages, with good reason. She'd seen Leah after several of them, when Thomas was still alive but too busy gambling to notice or care what his brother was doing to his wife. Leah knew it took a great deal of courage for her to confront him like this, and she had never loved her more.

"Yes, Mama, I'm fine. I'll be right there. Sir Horatio was just leaving." She pulled ineffectually at her arm, and after a moment of struggle Sir Horatio let go and Leah stumbled back.

"Do not forget what I said, Leah," he warned her, turning to leave. "I shall come to collect you in the carriage."

And I shall not be here, Leah thought defiantly, glaring at his back. *I will be with Valentine and Kurt, securing a future for myself and my children.*

~

That night Leah had trouble sleeping. It was hardly a surprise. She went over and over her discussion with Valentine and Kurt. She meticulously outlined, in her head of course, the advantages and disadvantages of such an alliance. In number the disadvantages were greater—ostracism, potential arrest for Valentine and Kurt if their relationship was exposed, always being wary, hiding the nature of their arrangement.

She couldn't help but dwell on the most selfish disadvantage, the fact that she would never be loved. Oh she believed that they liked her well enough, they certainly desired her. But Valentine and Kurt were in love with one another. She was merely a means to an end for them. After their meeting today she didn't think it immodest to say a pleasant means, but a means nonetheless. There was still a foolish, womanly part of her that longed to be loved. She wanted flowers and poems and declarations of undying love. She'd never had that and she wanted it so much it was an ache in her chest. Worst of all she thought she'd want it from Valentine and Kurt, and she knew she'd never have it. And there was the biggest disadvantage of all, a lifetime spent longing for what they could never give her.

While the advantages were not as numerous as the disadvantages, in importance they far outweighed them. Number one of course was the financial security marriage to them would provide. After three years of hellish poverty Leah couldn't underestimate the importance of that. The future provisions for the children were generous in the extreme and would alleviate a great burden from Leah. She also believed marriage to Valentine and Kurt would be pleasant. They were handsome, intelligent, kind and clearly heroic if one took into account their war service. No, marriage to men such as they would not be a burden. And she knew, after only a few short hours of acquaintance, that they would never abuse her or the children. Which brought her to what might be the greatest advantage—freedom from Sir Horatio.

Leah had been so young when she married. Thomas Marleston had been a pleasant enough young man, with a modest income, a sunny disposition and lively conversation. Leah had not loved him, but to her young mind marriage represented security, something that had been lacking in her life since her father's death. It took less than a year for Thomas to grow bored with his young, pregnant wife and seek his pleasure elsewhere. He did not, however, turn to another woman. Instead he turned to gambling. At first he was moderately successful, returning home with little trinkets for Leah purchased with his winnings. Most of the money was reinvested, as he called it, by paying for his next gambling venture. For the next several years it was a constant cycle of up and down, selling her jewels one day to buy new the next.

When Leah became pregnant with Esme she pleaded with Thomas to stop gambling. They had enough at that point to live modestly on the interest of what money they had, supplemented by a small allowance provided by his older brother. Sir Horatio had inherited all of their father's wealth and remained unmarried. Thomas had ignored her pleas, eventually returning home only rarely in order to avoid her censure. One year before his death Thomas had finally gone bankrupt. He'd pleaded for his brother's assistance, and Sir Horatio had allowed them all to move into his home. It was supposed to be a temporary arrangement, but Leah soon realized that Thomas had no intention of ending his gambling. Now that he didn't have to worry about providing for Leah and the children he gambled more heavily and lost just as heavily. He was never home and it didn't take long for Sir Horatio to start abusing Leah.

It started slowly, an unpleasantly firm grip on her arm if she displeased him in some way. Perhaps dinner was not to his liking, or the manor was not clean enough. He was always taking her to task for her inability to control the servants. Then he began finding fault with her person. She was too fat, too thin, too lazy. Her clothes were too tight, she was too loose, and so on. She complained to Thomas when he finally came home after the abuse had gone on for several weeks, escalating each time. His response had shocked her.

"Well, it is his household after all, Leah. You must strive to please him."

"But, Thomas, he is hurting me. Do you understand? Look,

look at this bruise." She showed him her arm, which had a dark purple bruise around the wrist. When he'd twisted it she'd thought at first he was going to break it. "And last week he slapped me. Slapped me, Thomas! In front of the servants." Leah started to cry.

"Oh stop your sniveling, Leah. Many was the time my mother could hardly walk for the beatings she took from Father, and she never cried about it. She just tried harder to please him. I expect Horatio is like him, he has a very exacting nature. He expects the best from everyone. You'll simply have to adjust." He'd left the next day.

Leah's greatest fear was for the children. She almost never allowed them to leave the nursery, and took to hiding there herself when she could. Thank God Sir Horatio had little use for them and preferred they stay out of his way. Leah had no one to turn to, nowhere to go. Her mother was scared of Sir Horatio and had very little income from her father's estate. With no brothers or cousins or uncles, Leah was adrift, drowning in fear for herself and her children. Then Thomas was killed, knifed to death in an alley in a London stew.

The day after Thomas' death Sir Horatio had finally pushed Leah into running. He had casually mentioned that they would marry as soon as her period of mourning was over.

"W-what?" Leah had stammered, her heart trying to pound its way out of her chest.

She had thought Sir Horatio a devil before, but the words he spoke then chilled her to the bone. "I knew as soon as Thomas came to me with his gambling debts that it was only a matter of time before his unsavory pastimes resulted in his death, either by someone else or his own hand. I've bided my time this past year, Leah, although both you and I know you became mine as soon as you entered my house. Why else do you think I've been training you this past year? All my little corrections, my dear, were in order to prepare you to be my wife." He had reached out and touched her cheek affectionately, as if his abuse had been a sign of his esteem for her. "You are quite pretty, Leah, and I shall not be embarrassed to take you as my wife. Society will think it only proper that I care for you and my nephew and niece now that Thomas is dead. I'm sure you will strive to please me." Her mind had flashed back to that earlier conversation with Thomas, and his casual mention of his mother striving to please his father, and being beaten down for her efforts. Horatio had pulled her to him roughly and kissed her, all open, slavering mouth and Leah had wanted to retch, too frightened of him to shove him away. It was he who finally pushed her away. He was panting with lust and Leah's stomach heaved. "You have teased and provoked me for a year, Leah, but I have resisted. I took care of you and the children and Thomas' debts and now I shall have my due. As soon as your mourning is over, we shall wed. Then you will truly be mine."

Leah had managed to convince Sir Horatio that until their marriage she should stay with her mother. Now that she was a widow and he an unmarried man it was improper for her to live with him. She had gotten unexpected support in this from the Duchess of Ashland, a dragon for the proprieties and a woman on whom Sir Horatio fawned. And so Leah had escaped with the children to her mother's. For the last three years Sir Horatio had been browbeating her into marrying him. She adamantly refused. He had cut off all her funds and refused to satisfy Thomas' debts, leaving them to her. He had recently coerced most of the shop-keepers in Ashton on the Green to refuse her any more credit. Leah believed the Duchess was behind that last attempt to force her hand.

By the time Valentine and Kurt had arrived with their offer Leah was at her wit's end. She had had no idea how to support her family, no place to run, nowhere to turn for succor. Now she had them. Whether or not they realized it, they were a dream come true.

CHAPTER 5

"*A*re you awake?"

Valentine's whisper came to Kurt in the dark, and he felt the heat of his body as Valentine rose on one arm to lean over him. He opened his eyes and saw the broad outline of Valentine's shoulders limned in moonlight.

"Yes, I'm awake." He had been. It was impossible to sleep, knowing that tomorrow their entire future could change, probably would change. There was no reason why Leah should not agree to marry them.

Valentine lay back down next to him, not touching him. "You haven't really said anything about her," he said quietly, the statement clearly meant as a question.

"Neither have you." Kurt tried to keep his tone neutral.

"I like her. I think I could love her." Valentine's tone was equally neutral.

"Good." Kurt tried not to let his tangled emotions show.

Valentine sighed. "'Good'. What does that mean?" He rolled onto his side facing Kurt. "Isn't this what you wanted? Talk to me, Kurt, tell me how you feel."

Kurt's frustration escaped when he answered. "How do I feel?

How the hell am I supposed to feel, Valentine? You tell me you could love someone else. Where does that leave me?" He raised both hands and scrubbed his face impatiently. "Damn. This is not turning out at all as I had planned."

Valentine gave a mirthless bark of laughter. "I was just telling myself that," he commented wryly. "Exactly how is this not like you had planned?"

It was Kurt's turn to sigh. "I believed that you could marry a woman without having strong feelings for her. I see now that that would be impossible for you. I didn't realize that I would feel so jealous."

"Kurt," Valentine said, and Kurt felt his hand smooth over his chest. As always, Valentine's touch made Kurt's heart pound and his cock began to grow hard. "You know I love you. I will always love you. Whatever feelings I have for Leah won't change that."

Kurt put his hand over Valentine's as it ran slowly up and down his chest and skimmed over his taut stomach. "I know. I'm just confused. I want you to be happy."

"*You* make me happy," Valentine told him quietly then leaned over and kissed Kurt's shoulder. Kurt's breath hitched. "I want you," Valentine whispered.

"Yes," was all Kurt said, and Valentine rolled on top of him. Lust surged through Kurt like a bolt of lightning as soon as he felt the hot slide of Valentine's skin against his own from chest to foot. Valentine wedged himself between Kurt's thighs, spreading his legs almost as if he were a woman, and then with a subtle undulation he brought their two hard cocks together. Kurt's breath hissed out as he thrust up with his hips.

"This is where you are, Kurt," Valentine told him, his lips barely touching Kurt's as he spoke. He levered himself up on his hands, forcing their cocks even closer together, and Kurt moaned. "Here, in my bed, in my arms." Valentine began to rock his hips into Kurt, creating a heated pressure and friction of cock on cock. "You're mine and always will be."

37

"Yes, Valentine, yes." Kurt couldn't remember wanting Valentine this much ever before, as if he would die if Valentine didn't fuck him soon. "Kiss me, Valentine," he pleaded, and reached up a hand to clutch the back of Valentine's head and pull him down.

Valentine chuckled darkly. "You want me desperately, don't you, Kurt?" He didn't wait for an answer. Instead he swooped down and captured Kurt's mouth. The kiss was instantly hot and demanding. Valentine invaded his mouth, tasting, licking and biting. It was a kiss meant to inflame, and it did. Valentine moaned into his mouth, and Kurt knew he was as much a victim of the kiss as Kurt.

Valentine broke away from the kiss with a groan. "Christ, I think I can't want you more, and yet each time I do. I can't imagine this changing between us, Kurt. Bloody hell, I want to fuck you." Valentine ran his lips down Kurt's jaw and neck and then bit the strong tendon of his shoulder gently. Kurt groaned.

"Yes, darling, I love to hear you. Tell me what you want, Kurt." Valentine scooted down and his teeth grazed Kurt's hard nipple before his tongue began to lash it. Kurt moaned loudly, knowing how much Valentine loved to hear him during their lovemaking. The more he could make Kurt moan and groan, the more he liked it. Valentine was a very vocal lover as well. Almost every one of Kurt's moans Valentine answered with one of his own.

"I want to fuck," Kurt gasped as Valentine began to suck his nipple vigorously. "I want your cock in me tonight, Valentine. I want you to own me, to control me, to fuck me hard and fast."

Valentine moaned and gave Kurt a series of light bites across his chest to his other nipple and began to suck that one as deeply as he had the other.

"*Meine Gott*," Kurt moaned, clutching Valentine's head to him. "Yes, suck harder, darling, suck me everywhere."

"Christ," Valentine muttered after he pulled away, "yes," and he moved lower, sucking and nibbling Kurt's stomach. He licked the length of Kurt's cock, and Kurt cried out wordlessly. When Valentine took the hard, throbbing erection into his mouth, all Kurt could do was sob his name over and over. Valentine worked his mouth down to the root of Kurt's cock, not easy since he was large and wide, but Valentine had years of practice.

He savored the salty taste of Kurt's precum in his throat then he sucked deeply on Kurt's cock, and slowly pulled his mouth down and off. Kurt moaned incoherently, his head thrashing on the pillow. Valentine moved his mouth down and gently licked the soft expanse of skin between Kurt's cock and his sac, then bit it ever so softly, causing Kurt to shiver and moan yet again. God he loved that sound. It made his own cock throb and he felt it leaking. He licked again, this time lower, over Kurt's balls and then across and into the sweet, tight hole he wanted so badly. Kurt thrashed and begged, "Please, Valentine, please."

"I can't wait anymore, Kurt," Valentine growled. "I'm so hard to fuck you I ache."

He needed Kurt in a way he never had before. He needed to show him how much he loved him and wanted him. Usually it was Kurt making love to Valentine with his mouth and his hands, but tonight he had to make Kurt understand how important he was to Valentine, that there would always be a place in his life and heart for Kurt. Loving him was like breathing to Valentine. It was essential, it gave his life meaning. This is what he wanted to share with Leah too, and he knew he could, that they could.

"The next time I do this, Kurt," he told him as he climbed back up his body like a predatory cat, his voice rough, "Leah will be here. She'll be watching us." Kurt's back bowed as his hips thrust up and Kurt gave a guttural moan. "Mmm," Valentine purred, "you like the sound of that, don't you?"

Kurt was breathing heavily, his eyes shut tight when Valentine crouched above him face-to-face. "Open your eyes and see me," Valentine whispered, "really see me."

Kurt's eyelashes fluttered, and his gaze was unfocused when he first opened his eyes. Then he looked into Valentine's eyes for a long minute.

"I see you," he said quietly. "You are the same, the same man who has shared my bed for years."

"Exactly," Valentine whispered again. "The same man who loves you. You will lose nothing, Kurt, by letting Leah in. You will only gain. You will win another lover, another person who will need you and love you as I do."

"Ah, *liebchen*," Kurt sighed. "I am afraid. I am afraid of changing everything. I am afraid to love her because I think I could."

Valentine smiled and then lowered his head and kissed Kurt softly. "I'm counting on it," he told him. "Now roll over so I can fuck you."

Kurt rolled over eagerly. He loved being fucked as much as he loved to fuck. He loved everything about his physical relationship with Valentine. He couldn't help wondering if he would love to fuck Leah as much.

"On your knees, Kurt," Valentine ordered roughly, grabbing Kurt's hips and pulling him up. Kurt came easily to hands and knees and spread his legs to make room for Valentine between them. Suddenly he felt Valentine's mouth on his arse, licking at the tight bud there, first the broad flat of his tongue and then the tip teasingly dipping in. He gasped. Oh God, this was one of his favorite things, his favorite way for Valentine to prepare him to be fucked.

"Valentine," he moaned, pushing back in Valentine's face. He was rewarded by a swift, hot stab of tongue delving into him. Kurt bit his lip as the pleasure coursed through him. With the next invasion of Valentine's tongue Kurt threw back his head and groaned loudly and deeply. Valentine's chuckle sent a wave of sensation into the sensitized ring of muscles he was working with his mouth, and Kurt suddenly couldn't stop shivering. He was aching with want as he was stretched to take Valentine's cock.

"I need you, Valentine," he groaned, "I need your cock so badly. Fuck me now, please."

Valentine couldn't help but smile as he heard Kurt's plea, and he knew it was a wicked smile. He loved nothing better than to reduce Kurt to begging. His cock was so hard it was resting high and long against his stomach. He could feel it leaking. He couldn't resist one last thrust of his tongue deep into Kurt's channel, swirling it roughly. Kurt loved this so much Valentine had once made him come from nothing but a tongue fuck. He pulled his tongue out slowly, and Kurt groaned. He gave one or two small bites to the puckered skin there, then rose on his knees behind Kurt, his hands on Kurt's backside, spreading him wide.

Valentine looked down and very carefully pressed the tip of his leaking cock against Kurt's back entrance, spreading the moisture from his cock around the lip of the hole. "Tell me what you want, Kurt."

"I want you," Kurt pleaded, "I want your cock inside me." Without preamble Valentine thrust his thumb into Kurt. "God, Valentine! Now, fuck me now," Kurt cried.

Feeling that Kurt was ready, Valentine pulled his thumb out, making Kurt moan. "Mmmm," Valentine purred as he pressed just the tip into Kurt. "It's so good, Kurt. You're so hot and tight tonight, and you want me so badly. I want to fuck you slow and deep so it lasts." His words were accompanied by his slow press deeper and deeper into Kurt, who bloomed beneath him, his body welcoming Valentine like the familiar lover he was.

Valentine had to stop speaking as he was overwhelmed with sensation when he thrust the last few inches into Kurt. Kurt was so tight and Valentine was so hard it felt like his cock was being strangled and he loved it. He groaned and thrust his hips shallowly several times, making room for his cock deep in there, stretching Kurt a little more before he began to fuck him hard and deep.

Valentine ran his hands over Kurt's behind and up his back to his shoulders. He stretched himself out against Kurt's back, spreading Kurt's legs wider and pushing him down until Kurt's head and shoulders were on the bed, his buttocks tucked in tightly against Valentine's hips, Valentine's cock still buried to the hilt. Kurt groaned and shuddered, and Valentine felt an answering shiver race up his spine.

"I want to fuck you like this for Leah," Valentine whispered. "I want her to see how beautiful you are, how much you like it. I want you to teach her how to suck a man's cock, and how to take one in the arse."

Kurt fisted his hands against the bed and a small whimper escaped him at the same time Valentine felt his muscles tighten around his cock.

"You want her here, don't you?" He continued to whisper roughly as he rose to his knees again behind Kurt and grabbed his hips. He pulled his cock out of Kurt slowly, then thrust back in hard and deep. Kurt thrust back against him moaning. "You want her to watch me fuck you. What else do you want?"

Kurt was breathing heavily, his cheek pressed against the bed, his hands opening and closing. He groaned as Valentine pulled out and thrust in again.

"I want to fuck her," Kurt gasped. "I want to fuck her while you fuck me. I want to taste her first, while you taste me, then I want us all to fuck."

Valentine's stomach clenched at Kurt's words, and he couldn't control himself. He thrust hard and fast and deep into Kurt three, four, five times. Kurt's arms were stretched above his head, his buttocks meeting Valentine's hips thrust for thrust. Kurt was panting and his head was twisting back and forth against the covers. He was the picture of sexual submission as he let Valentine fuck him ruthlessly, and Valentine gloried in it.

"I want to suck your cock while she sucks mine," Valentine rasped, as he slowed his thrusts, still going deep. "I want to do it outside, in the garden, where anyone could walk by and see us. I could lie down on the bench there, and you can kneel over my face while Leah lies between my legs, and I want to taste your cum in my mouth as I come in hers."

Valentine's words made Kurt shiver and moan, and he felt his bottom tighten around the long hard cock fucking him. His climax was building, his balls were high and tight and tingling with the need to come.

"Fuck me hard, Valentine," he groaned out, "I'm going to come. Fuck me hard and come with me."

Valentine complied and Kurt met him thrust for thrust, loving the feel of the hard cock going deep, the slap of flesh against flesh. When Valentine fucked him like this he hit a spot inside that felt so good it almost hurt. Suddenly Valentine thrust deep and stiffened behind him, holding his hips still in a bruising grip as he cried out. Then Kurt felt the hot wash of his seed inside him, and Kurt came and came, his hips jerking against Valentine's hold as he felt his own release on his thighs and stomach.

Kurt lay replete on the bed, boneless and unable to move from his kneeling position. Valentine lay curled over him, breathing heavily, his stomach and chest plastered to Kurt's back with sweat and heat. These moments were almost as sweet as the fucking to Kurt, when Valentine was so exhausted from loving him and yet wouldn't let him go.

"So you think it will be even better with Leah, yes?" Kurt asked teasingly, his voice still shallow and his breathing fast.

Valentine laughed weakly from behind him. "Better than perfect? No. Just a different kind of perfect, I think."

"Yes," Kurt slowly agreed, thinking back on the fantasies he and Valentine had just shared. "I think so too."

CHAPTER 6

*L*eah nervously smoothed the skirt of her gown with shaking fingers as the carriage rolled to a stop in front of Cantley. She took several deep breaths, and when the footman opened the carriage door she was ready.

She had been impressed with Valentine's carriage and was equally impressed with Cantley. While not a palatial estate, the brick and stucco two-story home was obviously large, and on the outside it was well maintained. In the fading light Leah could make out both formal and informal landscape elements that even in their winter state were quite lovely. A fountain lay idle in the center of the gravel roundabout in front of the house.

She took the outstretched hand offered by the young footman. Leah had been impressed by her first encounter with some of Valentine's and Kurt's servants. They were everything that was proper in their manners and behavior. Leah was relieved. She hadn't known what to expect. This was so far out of the realm of her experience. Her stomach was in knots from excitement and trepidation.

Her perusal of the house was cut short when the front door opened to reveal not a servant but the master himself. Valentine stepped out under the portico and smiled welcomingly. "Mrs. Marleston," he said warmly, and Leah was glad he'd used her proper title and surname in front of the servants. She didn't want there to be more talk than necessary in the neighborhood.

"Mr. Westridge," Leah answered a little shyly, "it's so good of you to have me here."

Suddenly Kurt was at the door behind Valentine, grinning wickedly. "Why, Mrs. Marleston, as soon as we met we knew we must have you here as soon as possible."

Leah didn't miss the innuendo in his remark and she felt her cheeks heat.

"Kurt," Valentine admonished gently, but Leah could see the twinkle in his eye and her heart raced. "Come in," he invited, holding out his hand, and Leah stepped forward. When their hands met, Leah's gaze flew to Valentine's. Had he felt it too, she wondered, that wonderful hot slide of awareness? It felt as if the earth shifted just slightly, and Leah thought, *my life will never be the same again.* As she walked through the door and Kurt closed it behind her it all felt so right it almost frightened her.

"Leah?" Kurt asked quietly, stepping closer and laying a hand on her arm. "Are you all right?"

"Oh yes," she replied with a tremulous smile, "yes, I'm all right."

After the emotional undercurrents of her arrival, the evening progressed rather banally. They had a sherry before dinner and idly talked of the neighborhood—who was who, and who Kurt and Valentine should meet. The only thing that distinguished this dinner from any other Leah had attended was that it was just the three of them. When they went in to dinner Leah found that Valentine was sitting at the head of the table, she was sitting to his right and Kurt was directly on her right. She was a little disconcerted to be surrounded by them, but as dinner progressed with normal light conversation Leah relaxed.

"Tell us about yourself, Leah," Kurt asked after the last dish had been removed. The men opted to take their port in the dining room with her. She declined their offer of a glass and settled on another sherry. With her before-dinner drink and wine with dinner she was feeling very relaxed.

"Oh I'm very boring. My family is country bred on both sides. I grew up about thirty miles from here, in Sedgely. Our house was half the size of this one, and the grounds not nearly so impressive. My father was a kind, forgetful, playful man who adored my mother. His death in a hunting accident was a tragedy she never recovered from." Leah sighed. "I guess I haven't either."

Kurt was sitting forward, his arm leaning on the table, his chin in his hand. At her remark he reached out and brushed a stray lock of hair behind her ear and Leah shivered, her nipples puckering in awareness much to her surprise. She had never become aroused from such an innocent touch before. She immediately put down her sherry. Clearly she'd had too much already.

"I'm sorry, beautiful Leah." He smiled at her shiver. "Tell us about your marriage."

"My marriage," Leah mused. "Well, because we were alone, I think I married too young. I was only nineteen when I accepted the first offer made to me. Thomas Marleston was a good catch for a country-bred girl with very little dowry and no connections." She shrugged, not wanting to reveal the harsh and sometimes ugly aspects of her marriage. "We had two children together in a few short years. Thomas began to gamble irresponsibly, he died in rather mysterious circumstances, and I came to live with my mother."

Both men regarded her silently for a moment. In her nervousness Leah forgot her earlier decision not to drink anymore and she took a sip of her sherry.

Valentine sighed. "I think there is a great deal there that you are not telling us," he chided gently. "Why?"

"I don't know," Leah answered evasively. "My marriage was no different from hundreds, thousands, just like it."

"It was very different," Kurt argued, "because it involved you."

Leah blushed, and Kurt's fingers were suddenly there on her hot cheek, brushing the overheated skin softly. "So shy," he murmured. "Why are you here, Leah?"

She blinked rapidly several times, trying to focus on his abrupt question.

"Because you asked me?" she offered helpfully.

Valentine laughed at her response. "We did. But why did you accept?"

"I thought you wanted my answer," Leah said in confusion.

Kurt's fingers had moved from her cheek to her neck and were now smoothly brushing back and forth along her collarbone, which was exposed by the fashionably low square neckline of her pale violet gown. Leah's breath hitched in her throat.

"Tell us your answer," Kurt encouraged her, his voice a low seductive purr.

Leah cleared her throat delicately, almost overwhelmed by the desire to take Kurt's hand and press it firmly against her breast, against the hard aching nipple there, tingling with the feel of Kurt's soft caress. She looked over at Valentine, unsure of how to progress. If she was to marry Valentine, shouldn't he be the one touching her first? He was sitting back in his chair, the very picture of wealthy, self-satisfied complacence. The description made Leah smile, and Valentine tilted his head inquiringly. Leah answered before he could ask the question.

"I was thinking how self-satisfied you look, very opulent and indulgent." Valentine looked momentarily taken aback and then his laugh joined Kurt's deep chuckle.

"I look that way because that's how I feel." Valentine leaned forward, bracing both elbows on the table, and held her gaze, his face serious. Gone was the stammering lover of yesterday. "I love watching Kurt's hands on you, watching you respond to his touch. I can see your breathing getting just a little ragged, your pulse quickening in your throat, and it makes me want you both."

Leah became conscious of the things Valentine described, her breathing and her heartbeat, and both increased as his words sank in and Kurt's caresses became bolder. His fingers were now running lightly over the soft swells of her breasts above her neckline. Shivers raced across her sensitized skin at the feather light brush of his fingers.

"You haven't answered us, Leah. Tell us, will you marry us?" Kurt's tone was casual, almost disinterested, but one look in his eyes dispelled that notion. His gaze was intense, pinning her to her seat.

Leah made sure to make eye contact with each man as she gave her answer. "Yes, I'll marry you."

For a moment Kurt's hand stopped caressing her and he held it tightly in a fist before relaxing it again and resuming his gentle torment. Valentine leaned back in his chair with a relieved smile.

"Thank God," Valentine said with a shaky laugh. "We weren't sure, we couldn't be sure, and the uncertainty has been killing us."

"Really?" Leah asked, proud of how calm she sounded. Inside she was a bundle of nerves over the realization that she had just committed herself to these two men for life, and she knew so little about them. "By my being here I thought you'd have figured out my answer." She glanced at Kurt and smiled. "In spite of what you might think, I don't generally let men fondle me at the dinner table."

Both men laughed, but the atmosphere had changed subtly. Kurt suddenly ran his fingers down over her breast and her tight nipple, and Leah couldn't stop a little gasp from escaping.

"You say yes without knowing what we'll ask of you." Kurt's eyes rose from her breast to meet hers. "Perhaps you should wait until you've sampled our lovemaking before making a final decision."

The thought had Leah's heart racing and her eyes went wide. "Now?" she squeaked, and winced at how panicked her voice sounded. "I mean, here?"

"Kurt—" Valentine began, but Kurt cut him off.

"Yes now, although not necessarily here in the dining room." He cut his gaze to Valentine. "It's best to find out now if she likes it, Valentine, rather than after the wedding, when it will be too late if she finds it's not to her taste."

Leah's eyes were darting back and forth between them, her mind a blank as to what she should say. If she said no, they might think she was not willing to share a bed with them both, and their offer may be rescinded. If she said yes, she was committing herself to this marriage of three, a relationship that flew in the face of everything society dictated was right and proper. For God's sake, her *husbands* would be each other's lovers, were lovers now. A day ago the idea was inconceivable. Now it was her future. And even more surprising was that the idea didn't scare her as much as it ought. In fact, it didn't scare her at all.

She'd had a marriage condoned by society, a good marriage by their standards, and it had been only tolerable at the best of times and a nightmare when Thomas had been gambling and Horatio had stepped into the void with his cruelty and possessiveness. She knew in her heart these two men were nothing like her dead husband and his brother. They would never be cruel and hurtful or neglectful.

Leah pulled her mind back to the conversation and suddenly realized Valentine was stammering in his endearing way again. Apparently he'd taken her silence as a denial. Kurt had retreated into himself, his face unreadable. Already Leah knew this was how they both responded to adversity. It was amazing how much she did know about them already, after knowing them only a day. How had she become so comfortable around them, so attuned to their feelings and desires? A sudden irrational thought brought her up short. Perhaps she'd always known. Perhaps she'd been made for these men, for this life, and she'd only been waiting for them to find her. She smiled at such a fanciful thought.

"Valentine," she said quietly, "the answer is yes, to the marriage proposal and to Kurt's suggestion. He's right, we need to find out if we are all comfortable with the arrangement before we make it permanent."

Her statement silenced both men, Valentine in shock and Kurt in assessment. "Are you always so practical?" Kurt asked her.

She had to smile. "About most things, yes, although it would seem there is very little of the practical about what you ask of me."

Valentine cleared his throat and stood. "Well then, I guess, would you like to go upstairs?"

Before Leah could answer him Kurt spoke. "I think it would be best if we went into the drawing room. The servants will talk already, but we should not give them more ammunition."

"Of course, of course," Valentine said abruptly, shaking his head at his own poor suggestion. "Not the bedroom. Of course."

Leah placed a hand on his arm. The heat and hardness of his muscled forearm beneath her palm had her sex clenching in anticipation, and Leah felt her mouth tilt in that age-old secret woman's smile. "Valentine, it's all right, relax. I'm nervous enough for us all." She took a deep breath and jumped off the precipice. "You see, I have absolutely no idea what...or...or how..." She trailed off, embarrassed again. "I know I want to, I think, but I'm not sure what I want to do." She scrunched her nose, a habit left over from a shy youth. "Does that make sense?"

At her admission Valentine's nervousness disappeared. He got up and pulled out her chair, lending a hand to help her rise. "In that case, let us go so we can show you."

CHAPTER 7

$\mathcal{T}$he walk to the drawing room was as excruciating as it was exciting. Valentine held her hand on his arm, his thumb stroking over her skin like a kiss. Kurt followed behind, a hot, imposing presence stalking them. Leah's skin felt overly sensitive, as if she could feel their eyes and their breath caressing her. It was her vivid imagination, she knew, but it was thrilling just the same. She'd never been so aroused in her life, and they'd hardly even touched her yet.

Kurt gently closed the door behind them and Leah heard the lock snick into place. She waited for the fear to come, but all she felt was excitement and arousal like a buzz in her head. Valentine brought her over to the settee. He turned her to face him, still standing, and kissed her on the cheek. The kiss spoke more of carnality than camaraderie. "What do you wish to know?" he asked her, his nose trailing softly over her hair and then down to her neck where he buried it in the curve of her shoulder. Leah felt a soft hot swipe of his tongue on her tendon there, and froze for a moment before heat sizzled along her nerve endings, straight to her sex where a dull insistent throbbing commenced.

Kurt walked over and took his place behind Leah, only this

time he pressed close against her, touching from his chest against her back to the hard ridge of his cock along the top curve of her bottom. He leaned over her free shoulder and whispered in her ear.

"What do you want to learn first, Leah love? How to fuck two men at once? Or how men make love? Would you like to watch Valentine and me fuck each other?"

Leah moaned, she couldn't help it. She had never heard such talk before in her life, and definitely not directed at her. Vague, unbidden images of what he described flashed in her mind, and her body temperature rose until she felt flushed and out of breath.

"Fuck?" she whispered. "Is that what it's called?" Valentine's hands slid down from her waist and around to gently squeeze her buttocks, and Leah's legs became weak. She sagged slightly between them, and Valentine's hands tightened while Kurt's hands gripped her waist high, nearly touching the bottom curve of her breasts. She found herself wishing fervently that he would touch them, fondle them. She suddenly realized her acquiescence had little to do with practicality and everything to do with a primal kind of desire she had never felt before. She wanted them, really wanted them.

"I can see we'll have to teach you the vocabulary of love, my dear," Valentine told her in between placing light kisses on her neck and shoulders, making her tremble in pleasure. "Making love is also called fucking, although not in polite company." The last was said with more than a trace of amusement. "Did your husband never use words on you?"

"Use words on me?" Leah's voice was low and halting as she felt Kurt's hands begin a slow inexorable glide up to her breasts. He covered them, cupping and molding them in his big hands, and Leah gasped as her back arched. She'd never dreamed a man's hands there could be so exciting.

"Words to arouse you," Valentine explained. "Hearing the words can be almost as exciting as the act itself." Valentine leaned back and watched Kurt caressing her breasts, and Leah became more aroused, the act more carnal just because Valentine watched. "I love watching Kurt touch you. You have beautiful breasts. I want to see them naked, I want to suck and lick them, and watch Kurt take your nipples in his mouth, nibble them and tongue them."

"Oh dear God," Leah groaned. Valentine's words made her sex clench yet again and her breasts literally ache for what he described.

"Do you see?" Valentine whispered. "How the words can enhance your pleasure? You like them, don't you?" His voice was knowing, the question rhetorical. Leah's pleasure was obvious to all of them, her mounting desire like a wave of heat surrounding them.

Kurt's clever fingers found Leah's aching nipples and plucked them roughly, making her shudder as the sweet sting traveled directly from her breasts to her woman's entrance. "You are too desirable not to fuck, Leah," Kurt whispered from behind her, his breath hot and moist against her nape. "Your body is crying out to be taken, it wants a hard cock, doesn't it? But we'll do it your way, Leah. Whatever you want, tonight. Tell us what you want."

Leah was swamped with want, she couldn't make her mind grab onto any one thing. She had so little experience, and just a few minutes with these two incredible men had shown her there were pleasures out there she had no notion of. She leaned her head back in agitated surrender, and it lay on Kurt's shoulder as Valentine took advantage and feasted with lips and tongue on her exposed neck.

"What do you want, Leah?" Kurt's voice had become synonymous with temptation to Leah. He was the devil whispering of her fall from grace, and all she could do was follow him to her downfall.

"I don't know," she panted, her breath hitching on a sob as Valentine's kisses went lower and he licked a path across the upper slopes of her breasts. "I don't know! Thomas…it was never like this, never. He came at night, in the dark, he put it in me and he left. What is this? What are you doing to me?"

"We're making love to you, Leah, properly, the way a woman like you should have it. We're worshiping your beautiful body, loving you with words and touches. We will fuck you properly too, in the light with hot, sweaty, naked bodies straining together and cries of ecstasy. This is what we offer you. Take it, take us. Love us, Leah, and let us love you."

Kurt's impassioned promises beat against all Leah's fears, conquering them. They called to her most wicked fantasies, ones she hadn't even known she had until yesterday. "Yes, yes, please," she cried out, "that's what I want, oh God, yes, please."

At Leah's reply, Kurt stepped back and she felt him loosen her dress. He pushed it down to her hips as Valentine stepped back to give him room. Once the men's heat and hardness was no longer pressing on her Leah was able to think a little more clearly. She allowed them to take her dress off, but then she stepped to the side, away from them.

"You," she told them, her voice trembling, "I want to see you both. I've never seen a completely naked man. I want to see what I'm getting."

Valentine was taken aback by Leah's request. She'd seemed overwhelmed by their passionate lovemaking. He'd assumed she'd let them take the lead. He liked her courage, and her obvious desire for them pushed his own arousal higher, hotter. He didn't want a meek bedmate, he wanted a woman who equaled him and Kurt in passion. She appeared to be a lady who, despite her lack of experience, knew what she wanted after all.

Valentine shrugged off his coat without even answering her. Her eyes widened and she licked her lips. The shine of the moisture on her lips made Valentine's mouth water. He unbuttoned his waistcoat quickly and threw it off, uncaring where it went. Leah's breathing was ragged. Next came his neckcloth. He realized his own breathing was less than steady as he absorbed Leah enjoying his hasty undressing, her desire growing. He watched her eyes dart to Kurt and he followed her gaze.

Kurt had also begun undressing and Valentine waited until the other man caught up with him before removing anything else. When Kurt's neckcloth floated to the floor beside him the two men shared a glance. They didn't need to speak to understand one another. They would undress together now, revealing themselves to Leah at the same time.

They both took off their shirts, and Leah gasped. "Stop," she whispered. She took a step closer and then hesitated. "May I touch you?" she asked.

Kurt laughed and Valentine smiled. "Yes, *leibchen*, touch all you want," Kurt told her, his voice deep with need. He reached out and Leah placed her hand in his. Kurt guided it to his chest, and he rubbed her hand over his hard muscles, then over his nipples, already sharp with arousal. The caress had him slowly arching his neck in pleasure.

"Do you like that?" Leah asked tentatively. "When I touch you there?"

Kurt raised his head again to look at her, and Valentine didn't need to see his face to know how he looked. He'd seen Kurt aroused so many times it was an image burned in his memory. He was beautiful that way, sloe-eyed with desire, his cheeks flushed, his movements slow and deliberate.

"I want you to touch me everywhere, my Leah. My nipples, my cock, my behind," he told her, and with each word he moved her hand on him to the places he named. Leah inhaled sharply when he pushed her hand deep between his legs and onto his backside. Kurt chuckled darkly and let her pull it away. "Perhaps not all tonight, but eventually," he said with a wolfish grin.

Leah stumbled back, and Valentine stepped over to catch her, her back against his bare chest. He wrapped his arms tightly around her, grabbing her hands so that she hugged herself with him, effectively held captive. He placed his lips against her ear as he spoke. "That's how we do it, Leah. That's how a woman fucks two men, and how men fuck each other—in the behind. It feels so good, sweetheart, so hot and thick and wonderful to be fucked there. It's what we'll do to you after we're married, and what we do to each other."

"Oh my God," Leah whispered brokenly, and the slight jerk of her hips let Valentine know she was aroused by the thought rather than frightened. She watched Kurt with wide eyes, her new knowledge written on her face. Kurt slowly unbuttoned his pants and pushed them down just enough to free his swollen cock. It sprang free and bounced against his stomach. Kurt was so hard Valentine knew he must be in pain. Leah whimpered and her legs collapsed beneath her.

Valentine swept her up in his arms and carried her to the settee, laying her down there. He and Kurt quickly divested themselves of the rest of their clothes while Leah stared at them with wonder. When they were naked, Valentine hesitated. "What do you want us to do, Leah?" he asked her, hungry to please.

She looked at them and licked her lips again. It was a nervous habit that pushed Valentine to the edge. He loved a tongue on him, licking and swirling everywhere it went. At her next words, he knew exactly what he was going to do.

"Show me," Leah told them. "Show me how you both like to be touched. Show me how to please you."

Valentine turned and beckoned Kurt to him with an outstretched hand.

Kurt knew what Valentine wanted, what he always wanted— Kurt's mouth on him. Valentine loved the hot wet swirl of a tongue on his skin, and Kurt loved the taste of him. He eagerly took Valentine's hand, lowering his head to lick along Valentine's shoulder before the other man could even speak. Valentine shuddered and groaned and Kurt smiled wickedly, his eyes meeting Leah's over Valentine's shoulder. Her eyes were wide, the pupils enlarged until they nearly blotted out the pale blue.

"Valentine loves to be licked, Leah, everywhere. He loves a mouth savoring him, teasing him with lips and tongue and teeth." Kurt turned Valentine slightly so Leah had a side view and could see everything that Kurt did to him. Kurt lowered his head and slowly licked across Valentine's hard nipples with the flat of his tongue. Valentine gripped the back of his head, fisting Kurt's hair and holding him there on one nipple. Kurt bared his teeth and bit down, lightly scoring his teeth along the aroused pebble, and Valentine groaned again, louder this time.

Kurt spoke with this lips still touching Valentine. "Valentine is a vocal lover. Not just the words, which he loves to speak and hear, but the sounds of sex. He can't control himself and is given to loud moaning. He also loves to hear his lover. He is happiest when he has driven me to the edge and I can't control my own moans. I like this too, it pleases me and heightens my own desire." He turned his head and rubbed his hair along Valentine's nipple with a slight repetitive motion of his head while he looked at Leah. "I want to hear you in your passion too, Leah. I want to hear you moan and sob for us, beg us to fuck you. Never be embarrassed to express what you're feeling when we make love to you."

"Kurt." Valentine's voice was a growl. "Lick me down, and then suck my cock. Show Leah how good you are at that." Kurt's stomach clenched as he remembered similar words from Valentine last night.

Leah moaned out loud and Kurt laughed. Valentine looked at her, and Kurt could see she was as affected by the dark passion in his face as Kurt was. "Was it the words that made you moan, Leah, or the thought of what I want him to do?" Valentine asked.

"Both," Leah said breathlessly.

"What do you want right now, Leah?" Valentine's voice was harsh and his breathing erratic as Kurt licked down his stomach, paying special attention to his hips and the crease between his legs and his crotch. "Do you want to touch me, or touch yourself?"

Leah gasped and Kurt looked up at her. "Don't be embarrassed, beautiful Leah. It would give us great pleasure to watch you touch yourself."

Leah was sitting up on the settee and she had her arms wrapped around her waist. She bit her lower lip, staring at them in anguish for a minute before she spoke. "I don't know how to begin."

"Bare your breasts for us, Leah, and fondle them. Whatever gives you pleasure. Show us what you like." Kurt waited, trying not to let his impatience show. He burned for this, to see Leah rubbing her own breasts, putting her fingers in herself, coming as he sucked Valentine. It was best, he thought, this first time that she pleasure herself to their passion before they touched her. It would relax her, and she would be wet and ready for a cock then.

"Yes," Valentine groaned, "God yes, Leah, please."

She reached for the ties on her corset, and Kurt grinned in triumph.

CHAPTER 8

*L*eah couldn't believe she was going to do this, touch herself in front of two men. But then everything about this evening seemed like a dream. Two days ago she never would have imagined watching two men make love, and enjoying it. More than enjoying it, actually, if she were honest with herself. She hungered for it, she was devouring their passion for one another. She wanted to do the things Kurt was doing to Valentine. She wanted to do it to both of them, and the reality was she would, and that excited her beyond measure.

As she removed her clothes to bare her breasts, Leah was brutally honest with herself. She was going to touch herself not because it would give her pleasure but because it was what Valentine and Kurt wanted. She supposed for them it was like her watching them now. She really couldn't imagine getting that much pleasure from her own hands. After she was bare to the waist, Leah looked up at them.

"*Meine Gott*, you are beautiful," Kurt whispered. His face was flushed, his eyes burning bright, and Leah felt beautiful.

"Do it, Leah," Valentine whispered and she looked at him. His face was all angles, sharp and harsh with desire. "Touch your breasts. Let us see you."

She could feel her face flame in embarrassment, but she made her hands cup her breasts and squeeze them. She gasped at the sensation. It felt good, very good, and she began kneading them and running her palms over her distended nipples. She had to bite her lip to keep from crying out.

While she fondled her breasts, she continued to watch the two men. Kurt placed one hand around Valentine's muscular thigh and then wrapped the other around the base of his cock. Keeping his eyes on Leah, watching her watch him, he leaned forward and guided Valentine's cock to his mouth. His tongue flicked out and licked the shining plum head of Valentine's very thick cock, and Leah actually moaned at the sight. Kurt smiled.

"Very good, Leah. Let me hear your pleasure. I like your moans." Kurt placed his smiling mouth against the end of Valentine's cock then, slowly opening his lips, he took the cock deep in his mouth. Leah sobbed at the desire that flamed through her, roughly squeezing her breasts. The vision before her combined with her own caresses had her sex aching and wet.

Valentine hissed as Kurt slowly pulled back along his cock, releasing it. Kurt began to lick around the thick shaft, and Leah saw Valentine shiver at the sensation. He clutched Kurt's head in his hands, fisting his hair, and turned eyes smoky with passion to her. "Show me, Leah," Valentine begged her, his voice rough with desire. "Show me how wet you are, how much you like what we're doing."

"Show you?" Leah gasped, pinching her nipples roughly as Kurt had done earlier. The feeling was a sort of painful pleasure that she liked.

"Your sex, your mound," Valentine panted as Kurt once again swallowed his cock.

Leah blushed again but rose and took off the rest of her clothing. Kurt stopped what he was doing to look with Valentine, and Leah saw stark male appreciation in both faces. She wasn't sure what to do next until Valentine spoke again.

"Sit down again, Leah," he told her, "and spread your legs wide so we can see your sweet, wet slit. I know you're wet for us. Do you ache to be fucked yet, Leah?"

Valentine's words made Leah sink back on the settee, her legs wide, her sex indeed aching. "I've never felt like this before, Valentine. Is that what it is? Do I ache to be fucked? My body is a stranger to me tonight." She heard the tremor in her voice and raised her hands to her breasts again, trying to relieve some of the tension she could feel building.

Kurt spoke, still on his knees before Valentine, the other man's cock still in his fist. "Touch yourself, Leah. Feel the heat, the wet. This is what desire really is. You were made for a cock, you want it."

His voice had the deep, mesmerizing tone that beckoned her to the forbidden, and she obeyed. She moaned at how wet she was, how sensitive. She ran her fingers up and down her crease, feeling how swollen her lips were there, how hot the aching flesh felt. She circled her weeping entrance.

"Put it in," Valentine whispered. "You know you want to, Leah. Fuck yourself with your finger."

Leah pushed her finger inside and cried out at the relief she felt at filling that empty, aching space.

"Suck me, Kurt," Valentine commanded roughly. "Suck me until I come, until you swallow all of me. Then I want to watch you fuck Leah."

"Oh God, oh God," Leah moaned, her eyes closing as she moved her finger. Everything was too much, she was so full, and so confused.

"Are you going to come, Leah?" Valentine asked her, and she opened her eyes to see Kurt's head moving up and down, his

61

mouth sliding along Valentine's cock. She felt her sex clench her finger at the sight, and the feeling was marvelous. She moaned.

"Kurt's beautiful mouth is so hot and wet, Leah," Valentine whispered, "just like your cunt. He sucks until it's so tight, and I fuck his mouth like I want to fuck you, like I fuck him."

Leah's cry was wild and she moved her finger harder and faster, trying to ease the ache.

"Yes, Leah, come for us," Valentine hissed.

"I don't know how!" Leah cried out, tears pooling in her eyes. "I don't know!"

"Sshhh, darling," Valentine whispered. "Have you never come before, love?"

Leah was shaking her head, watching Kurt suck Valentine's cock. She was shaking all over, her eyes wide, her finger working inside her, and Valentine arched his back in pleasure as he drove his cock deep in Kurt's mouth. Kurt moaned his approval, and Valentine could feel his own climax coming. He gritted his teeth and held it off. He wanted to watch Leah come first, her first time if he guessed correctly. He tightened his fists in Kurt's hair, stopping him, Valentine's cock still buried deep between his lips.

"Press your palm against the little button at the top of your crease, Leah," Valentine panted. "Press against it while you fuck your finger in and out. It will feel so good. You'll know when you come, my love. You'll know." Leah did as he directed and her moan told him she was doing it right.

"Oh my God, Valentine, oh my God," she cried out. Her breathing was fast and erratic, and Valentine could see when she stopped watching him and Kurt and instead began concentrating on the feelings she was giving herself. It was beautiful and so bloody arousing he was ready to come that instant.

Suddenly Leah hunched her back and threw back her head, her keening cry filling the air. Valentine hungrily watched her come, her satisfaction his own. "Yes," he whispered. He glanced down and shared a look with Kurt, and he knew his lover was imagining the same thing, Leah coming with them inside her. "Soon, Kurt darling, soon," he whispered and Kurt closed his eyes and sucked hard on Valentine's cock.

Valentine moaned and let himself go. He pumped in and out of Kurt's mouth, unable to contain the sounds of his own arousal. His balls were tingling, burning with the need to come. He felt the heat travel up his cock until it seemed as if pleasure exploded from the end deep in Kurt's throat. Valentine arched his back as the climax gripped him, crying out at the feel of Kurt swallowing around the end of his cock.

Kurt fell back, catching himself on his hands, breathless after Valentine's climax. God, he loved sucking Valentine, loved the taste and feel of him, his wild abandon when he came in Kurt's mouth. Watching and hearing first Leah and then Valentine come pushed Kurt to the edge. His cock was so hard it hurt. It felt as if he had never been this excited before, this desperate to fuck. He took a deep breath and rolled to his feet.

"My turn," he said, quickly crossing to the settee. He grabbed Leah's feet and raised them to the settee, turning her whole body in the process until she was lying down. He climbed on top of her and roughly spread her thighs wide with his knees. Only then did he look at her face. She was dazed, flushed prettily from her climax, her hair lying in wild disarray around her. She was so beautiful and desirable that Kurt's cock throbbed with the need to thrust deep within her. He met her eyes and froze.

"Leah?" he asked, hesitant. She was crying, silent tears slipping from her eyes to roll down her temples into her hair.

"What is it?" Valentine asked from where he was sitting down on the floor, still trying to catch his breath. He crawled over next to them and leaned over Leah. "My God, Leah, are you all right?"

Leah began to laugh through her tears. "Two children, and I never knew I could do that. That bastard."

"What?" Kurt asked, confused.

Leah looked at him, and wiped her eyes with the heels of her hands, like a child. "Thomas. He never told me, never took the time to let me. Come? Is that what that's called?"

Valentine grinned wolfishly from the floor. "It's called a climax, or orgasm. Or *le petite mort*, as the French say, the little death."

"How often can I do that?"

Kurt laughed out loud. "As often as you want. We can do that for you too. When we fuck, or when we kiss you down there."

"Kiss me…" Leah's eyes got very wide. "You mean like you did to Valentine?"

Kurt nodded. "Yes, similar. I like to do that to women too. You smell delicious, and someday soon, I'll do that. But right now I want desperately to fuck. May I fuck you, Leah?"

Valentine laid his arms along the cushion next to Leah's head and rested his chin on his crossed hands. "May I watch?"

Leah closed her eyes briefly, and when she opened them, Kurt saw desire and something else, something that made his heart quicken and his soul sing.

"Yes, darling Kurt. Please fuck me."

He needed no further encouragement. Without another word he found her entrance with his cock. She was so hot and wet Kurt shivered with anticipation. He slid inside her slowly, but with one smooth thrust to the hilt, and Leah moaned deeply in delight. Kurt had to take several deep breaths to gain control of himself.

"Tell me," Valentine whispered, staring at Kurt.

"She's so wet and hot, my love, so tight. I cannot last long, I think. She feels so wonderful." His accent grew thicker with his passion.

"Yes, I do," Leah whispered back, a trill of laughter in her voice. "I want to feel even better. *Le petite mort*, please."

Kurt couldn't stop his snort of laughter, and he saw Valentine grinning like a fool beside them. "We have created a monster, I think," Kurt told him. Leah laughed again.

Her laughter had a strange effect on Kurt. He felt his eyes fill with tears. This laughter, this wonderful closeness, would this be their future? Suddenly that future was bright and filled with promise, and Kurt felt lighter than he had since the war. Was this what Leah would bring them? God, he hoped so. He leaned down and buried his face in her neck, clutching her to him and thrusting deeper into her.

Leah gasped. "Kurt?" she asked breathlessly, concern in her voice.

He couldn't look at her. "Love me, Leah," he whispered. He felt Valentine's hand on his back, Valentine's lips on his shoulder as Leah ran a gentle hand through his hair.

"Yes," she whispered, "I think I shall."

She began to move beneath him, her movements untutored, and Kurt moved with her. He reached one hand down and firmly moved her hips in a smoother motion, showing her how to match him. When she caught the rhythm he pulled his head back from her neck with a gasp. Leah moaned at the exquisite feeling.

"There, yes," Kurt panted, his thrusts gaining in intensity and speed.

"Kurt," she said, over and over, like a prayer. He felt the same. It was perfect, everything about it. He'd never felt a fuck so right except for Valentine. Being in Leah was as good as being in Valentine—tight, hot, intense. Suddenly Leah's movements became more frantic, and Kurt knew she was close.

"Oh God," she cried, "it's going to happen again! Fuck me, Kurt, harder," she demanded, and he complied. He felt her muscles clamp down on him and begin to pulse almost before she began crying out as she climaxed. He held himself deeply inside her, pressing hard against her, trying to make her pleasure last, and then to his surprise without any further thrusts his climax came. His back arched with the force of it and he felt his seed shooting out endlessly, his body racked by shudders of ecstasy. Leah clutched him to her with arms and legs wrapped tightly around him, and then he felt her come again, not as hard but deeper, and she moaned.

"My God," he heard Valentine whisper. "That was beautiful."

CHAPTER 9

*K*urt collapsed atop Leah after his climax. His face was buried in the crook of her neck, his arms still wrapped possessively around her. Valentine felt tears on his cheeks and quickly wiped them away. He'd seen Kurt come many times before in many ways, most often with or inside Valentine himself, but this time was different. Before Kurt had always seemed almost melancholy afterward, his mood slightly dark. Valentine didn't doubt Kurt's love for him, but he'd known something was missing. This time Kurt had looked euphoric, sated, happy.

Thank God his plan had worked. When Kurt first mentioned the notion of taking a wife, Valentine had been surprised to say the least. But the idea had taken root in his mind and his heart. A wife who would bring children and softness and the kind of nurturing only a woman possessed. He needed that. He didn't have nightmares from the war, having Kurt had saved him from the war grief and madness that afflicted so many of his brothers in arms. But he lived with the memories every day and so did Kurt. They needed someone to help them start anew, a beginning that didn't come with death and violence.

Valentine knew from the start that Kurt believed he was doing it for Valentine, that he, Kurt, didn't need or want a wife. But Valentine knew Kurt better than he knew himself, and Kurt did need the laughter and light of a wife and children. Just a few hours with Leah, and Valentine could see the difference in him. Valentine had pretended to reluctantly go along with Kurt's plan, all the while hoping they could find a woman Kurt could love.

Then, in London, Valentine had confided in Stephen Matthews. Stephen had agreed with Valentine that Kurt's dark moods were getting worse. He also agreed a wife was a wonderful idea. And it just so happened, Stephen had offered with a wink, that he knew the perfect woman. Valentine thought Stephen had been joking or at least exaggerating, but after meeting Leah he realized Stephen had been completely serious. She was the perfect woman for them.

He owed Stephen a great deal, he thought with a smile, as he gazed with wonder at Leah's perfect profile, her strong chin and aristocratic nose. Her sensual mouth and those eyes, those pale blue eyes, bright with wonder and self-knowledge; she turned her head and those eyes were looking at him.

"Kiss me, Leah," he whispered. She leaned toward him and he raised himself on his knees to better reach her mouth. She was all willing submission and softness beneath his lips. He realized this was their first kiss. She opened for him at a slow swipe of his tongue on the plump curve of her lower lip, and he delved inside her mouth. He felt rather than heard her sharp intake of breath as his tongue met hers. Her hesitation and innocent response revealed her inexperience with this kind of soul kiss, a kiss Kurt had taught him.

Valentine went deeper into the kiss, applying more pressure with his lips, moving his tongue farther into her mouth, sucking as he played with her tongue. Leah moaned and moved one arm from Kurt to wrap it around Valentine's neck, hugging him close. Her hand dove into his hair and fisted it tightly, and Valentine felt his cock twitch in arousal again. Just as he began to entertain thoughts of another bout of lovemaking, perhaps fucking Leah himself, Kurt let out a gentle snore. Leah snorted into the kiss and pulled back with a quiet laugh, and Valentine let her, smiling.

"Our first kiss," Leah whispered, reading his mind.

"The first of many," Valentine assured her, leaning forward to kiss her forehead softly. "Rest for a bit, then we will see you home, my love."

~

*V*alentine roused Leah and Kurt after a short rest, as the hour was getting late and he wanted to take her home before her mother started to worry. Kurt was endearingly embarrassed that he had fallen asleep while still atop Leah, and inside her. Leah hadn't cared at all. It was wonderful—the weight of a hot, sated, naked man covering her, his cock still warm in her.

She felt like a different woman. She was a different woman thanks to these two men. She would never again settle for the kind of half-life she'd been living, now that she knew what she'd been missing. The smile was permanently attached to her face as she thought of all the wonderful years of fucking and coming ahead of her with Valentine and Kurt.

They were in the carriage with the lamps lit, and all three were squeezed onto one side, Leah in the middle. She was half draped over both of them, and Kurt was rubbing her feet while Valentine placed little kisses on her neck and nibbled on her ear.

"What are you grinning about, little cat?" Kurt asked quietly, and she opened her eyes to see him regarding her with a lazy smile, his own head resting on the back of the seat cushion.

"I've got the canary rubbing my feet," she answered just as lazily, and Valentine chuckled in her ear, sending sweet chills down her back.

"Mrs. Westridge," Valentine murmured, "you have a quick wit."

"The better to eat you with," she growled teasingly, and then laughed with the other two. She couldn't remember a time she had ever engaged in such silly banter with a man. Thomas had had no sense of humor at all.

She settled more deeply into the seat, snuggling back against Valentine and rubbing one foot on Kurt's thigh. "When will we marry, Valentine?"

"As soon as possible," he sighed, licking her neck right below her ear. She giggled. "I've got a special license already. I obtained it in London, hoping you would say yes."

"Sight unseen?" she asked lightly.

Valentine winced. "That seems so cold now that we know you," he admitted, "but Stephen said you would make a good wife to us, and marriages have been based on less."

"Oh I'm not upset," Leah hastened to assure them. "I'm planning on thanking Stephen profusely when he gets back." Both men smiled.

"Stephen returns from London on the fifth," Kurt said. "We can be married soon after." He grinned mischievously before adding, "Or we could have a longer engagement and get married on your birthday, Valentine. Very romantic."

Leah felt Valentine tense behind her, and she turned slightly to regard him with incredulous eyes. "Don't tell me?" she asked, laughter in her voice.

"Where on earth did you think I got the name?" he asked roughly. "Yes, February fourteenth, Valentine's Day." He jostled her so she was facing front again. "And I've bloody well had to endure enough teasing about it to last me a lifetime. And no, I'm not waiting months to marry Leah."

"Well, at least you wouldn't forget our wedding date," Leah teased, and Kurt laughed aloud as Valentine teasingly bit her earlobe.

"Where will we live?" Leah changed the subject.

"Well, we thought here, at Cantley." Valentine got a horrified

70

look on his face. "Surely you don't want to live in London, do you?"

Leah had to laugh at his expression. "No, not really, although I've never been and would like to visit one day. What's so horrible about London?"

Kurt had a very serious look on his face when he answered. "We're afraid London would be very bad for your health, my love."

"Is it so very dirty then?" Leah asked curiously.

"Yes, the refuse and air are bad particularly when combined with madmen running around assaulting our friends' wives."

"What?!" Leah was aghast at Kurt's comment. "What do you mean?"

"We have several friends in London who have married as we will, a marriage of three. One group made a very unfortunate enemy several years ago, and despite his rather outlaw status after attempting to kill one of them he managed to get back into the country. He has since attacked the wife of two other mutual friends."

"Oh my God!" Leah exclaimed. "Is she all right?"

"Now, yes, but she was rather badly beaten and frightened. I won't have you put at risk that way." Valentine's arms snaked around her more snugly, and his voice was hard.

Leah felt a frisson of fear. "Should I be worried?"

Kurt reached over and took her hand. "No, at least we don't think so. We believe we'll be well out of his sights here in the country, and would like to keep it that way."

Leah relaxed at Kurt's assurance. Then she focused on the most interesting part of his story. "There are others like us?"

"Yes, indeed there are, my dear," Kurt told her with a smile. "When we go to London you shall meet them, but not for a while."

Leah silently agreed. She had no desire to travel into danger if she could help it. The conversation made her think of their other friends. "What is the duke like?"

"Freddy?" Valentine sounded a little startled at the change of topic. "He's, well…he's Freddy."

Kurt laughed. "That says it all, and says nothing." He shrugged in his usual manner, the movement speaking volumes. "He is young and inexperienced, but a good man I think. He likes to laugh and that is always good in a peer."

"He must be very aware of his position if he is at all like his mother." Leah couldn't stop her moue of distaste.

Both Kurt and Valentine burst out laughing. "Freddy?" Valentine said with good humor. "No, he is nothing like that. Brett spends half his time reminding Freddy who and what he is."

"Brett?" Leah inquired.

"Brett Haversham. He's Freddy's constant companion. He was good friends with Freddy's older brother Bertram during the war, was injured in the same incident where Bertie died. Since he came back Freddy's hardly left his side."

Kurt's tone was neutral, so Leah had to ask. "Are they lovers, like you two?"

Kurt looked thoughtful for a moment. "No, I am sure they are not, although Freddy I think would like to be. But Brett, he puts Freddy off." Kurt shrugged again in bewilderment.

"Will he like me?" Leah didn't want Kurt and Valentine's friends to look down on them for their marriage to a simple country widow with children. Their friends sounded so sophisticated. No matter what they said, a duke was a lofty friend indeed.

"They will love you," Valentine assured her, kissing her neck, "if only because we do."

❧

"What the hell?" Valentine muttered behind her, and Leah opened her eyes. She'd dozed off to the rhythm of the carriage, in the security of both men's arms.

"What is it?" she asked groggily, sitting up and stretching. She followed his gaze out the window and saw the cottage ablaze with lights.

"Oh my God!" Leah was frantic. Something must be wrong. The cottage should be dark this time of night, the children in bed.

The carriage came to a halt, and Valentine threw open the door, jumping down and turning to lift Leah out. She ran for the door, Valentine and Kurt close behind her. Before she could reach it, the door flew open and Sir Horatio stepped out in her path. She barely had time to stop before his arm drew back and delivered a ringing blow to her cheek, knocking her down. She saw stars and lay there dazed for a moment.

"You filthy slut, I had to lie to the Duchess to cover up your whoring," he hissed. "I'm taking these children tonight. I will be back in the morning to discuss your punishment."

"You pathetic bastard," Valentine ground out, and Leah's vision cleared in time to see him haul Sir Horatio off his feet by his cravat. "Do you gain your pleasure by abusing those weaker than you? Do you dare take on a man instead of women and children?" Valentine held him suspended on his toes with one hand and backhanded him across the face with the other.

"You foul whoreson," Sir Horatio gasped. "You'll pay for that, and for what you and your foreign lover took from me tonight." Valentine threw him on the ground as if he were trash. The older man's face was livid with fury. "Leah was mine, mine. I was willing to marry her, but now I won't. She's not good enough now. I'll get everything I want without having to wed the whore. And you will be driven from the neighborhood, from England if I have my way."

Kurt and Mrs. Northcott had rushed to Leah's side as soon as she went down, and she now sat on the ground, her mother's arms around her. Kurt walked over to stand in front of Sir Horatio for a moment then he bent his knees to squat in front of the fallen man. His voice was all the more menacing for its quietness.

"It is you who will be leaving, Marleston, if you value your life.

By next week, Leah will be Mrs. Westridge. As of tonight both she and her mother, and the children too, will be at Cantley with us. You will never touch them or see them again. I will make sure the Duke knows of this incident, and you will no longer be welcome at Ashton Park. And yes, Valentine and I do have that power. You are through being the bully. There is nothing left for you here."

Kurt stood and turned his back on the older man, completely disregarding him as a threat. Sir Horatio was left gasping like a fish on the ground. Kurt turned to the door and saw Bastian and Esme there. "Come, *meine kinder*, let us go and pack your things," he said gently, and Esme let him pick her up and carry her inside.

Valentine picked Leah up in his arms and her mother hurried inside ahead of them. As he walked past Sir Horatio, Leah's head on his shoulder, he paused and looked down. "By the end of the week, or I will kill you," he said in a flat voice, and Leah didn't doubt his words. She buried her face in his neck and wrapped her arms tightly around him. She didn't want to see Sir Horatio ever again, not even lying on the ground in defeat.

"I think I will love you too," she whispered, looking up at Valentine after he kicked the door closed behind them.

He smiled down at her. "Of course you will, my dear. It's all part of the plan."

Sir Horatio was livid. He waited until the door closed and then started to rise. It was only then that his footman hurried over to help him. The man had been standing off to the side near Sir Horatio's carriage, hidden in the shadows. He'd wanted to surprise Leah when he confronted her with her treachery and perfidy. He hadn't counted on the two unnatural bastards being with her.

"Get away!" he snarled at the servant. He hoisted himself to his feet with difficulty, his tight corset making it hard to do. "I see you didn't rush to my assistance when I was being assaulted by that ruffian."

"Well, I…" the footman stuttered, clearly afraid to continue.

"Never mind, you fool," Sir Horatio ground out. "I don't need your assistance. I have my own ways of making them pay."

CHAPTER 10

*T*wo days later Leah and the children were settling in at Cantley nicely. Bastian and Esme were enthralled with the nursery, which contained some old toys left by the previous owners. Their pleasure at such tawdry cast-offs nearly broke Kurt's heart. He'd sent off two of the footmen to buy every toy available in the village. He was firmly determined to make them the two most spoiled children in Christendom.

Valentine had taken over Bastian's lessons until a tutor could be found. He'd sent off a notice to the *Times* and was hopeful he'd have some decent inquiries soon considering the salary he was offering.

And Leah was finally letting herself relax. Being free of worry was such a new concept to her she was having trouble adjusting. She'd actually pinched herself so hard that morning trying to make sure it was all real she'd left a bruise on her arm. She was also trying to learn how to take care of a household the size of Valentine's. Yesterday at breakfast she'd asked Valentine what would be required of her as his wife.

"You will take care of the house I should imagine," he'd told her vaguely.

Leah had sighed with impatience. "Yes, but what exactly does that entail, Valentine? How many servants do you have? Have you a housekeeper? Will I be responsible for the household accounts as well?"

He'd looked at Kurt, lost. "I, I don't really know Leah. Kurt handles all that."

Leah had seen then how it would be. "I see. And now I will too."

Valentine had smiled ingeniously. "Exactly, my love."

Kurt laughed. "Valentine wishes to have a pack of dogs and a stable of hunters, my dear, and perhaps a racehorse or two. And in his free time he shall also raise children. The other details of his life he leaves to you and me."

Rather than be annoyed Leah was euphoric. To be able to oversee a house like Cantley was a dream come true. She needn't worry about money, they'd made that clear. Between the two of them they were quite solid financially, their money invested well and growing daily.

She'd spent the morning with the housekeeper, as it turned out Valentine did indeed have one. She was a no-nonsense woman with a bit of a cockney accent and she made no secret of her origins with Leah.

"Mr. Westridge and Mr. Schillig hired me out of the stew," she told her baldly. "I ran my own house there with a few girls, but was needing to go on the up and up you see. They give me a chance, and a couple of my girls as well."

To say Leah was startled was putting it mildly. "I see." She decided to speak as plainly as Mrs. Cadwalter. "Will they be a problem, do you think?" She'd heard tales of street girls lying their way into a position in a good house only to pick up their old ways with the other servants and their masters.

"Not at all, mum," she'd firmly declared. "Hired us because they served with our misters they did. All died in the war you know. Looked us up to see how we were doing, and being the gentlemen they are offered us a better way. We'd never do nothing to embarrass them."

Leah was moved almost to tears. How like Valentine and Kurt to do something like that. She felt petty for thinking ill of these women for even a moment. She knew how hard it was for a widow with no means in this world.

"I'm quite glad to hear it, Mrs. Cadwalter," was all she said. "Shall we begin with a tour of the house?" Her head was spinning by teatime with all the information she'd received. Linens, menus, accounts, servants—she could hardly keep it all straight. She finally realized what it meant to be the wife of a wealthy man, and the responsibilities it entailed.

Leah took tea with her mother in the back garden. "I wonder if I should send someone for the boys," she muttered as she poured her mother a cup.

"Is that what we're calling them?" Marjorie said archly. "I wondered."

Leah slowly put the teapot down and looked at her mother. "I'm sorry. I guess I haven't really discussed anything with you. I failed to see that this affects you too."

Marjorie instantly put her cup down and took Leah's hand. "No, darling, I'm sorry. I didn't mean anything by that remark. It's just, this is rather…" She flapped her hands in the air and then gave up. "I'm not sure what this is quite frankly."

Leah bit her lip and contemplated a lie, but in the end opted for the truth. Her mother would be here quite a lot, even after she moved back to her cottage. She would figure it out eventually. Leah was uncomfortable with the idea of lying to her anyway. She'd stood staunchly by her side through her disaster of a marriage and the calamity of Thomas' debts.

"I'm going to marry Mr. Westridge," she started, "as soon as possible."

"I gathered that from Mr. Schillig's comments last night,"

Marjorie replied. "But what of Mr. Schillig? What is his role here?" Her look was shrewd.

"He is Valentine's lover and will be mine as well." Leah's voice was steady, her tone perhaps a touch defensive, but she felt her face flame as she spoke.

"I see." It was Marjorie's turn to be startled. She looked away for a moment. When she looked back she too was blushing, but she forged ahead. "And is this what you want?" She reached for Leah's hand again and gripped it tightly. "No one's forcing you? We can find another way to thwart Sir Horatio, if this is against your will."

Leah grabbed her hand with both of hers. "Oh no, Mama. This is what I want. They are both good men, and they need me. I care for them both already. True, I entertained their proposal at first because of our circumstances, and because almost anything was better than Sir Horatio. But now, now I can see a happy future here for me and the children. They are honorable men, and they respect me and care for me in return. We can make it work, we can."

Marjorie closed her eyes briefly, and when she opened them Leah saw the love and determination that had always supported her. "All right then," Marjorie said briskly. "If this is what you want, then we shall all make it work."

Leah leaned over and hugged her. "Oh thank you, Mama, thank you."

Marjorie cleared her throat and asked Leah about her morning. She was telling her all about Mrs. Cadwalter when they were interrupted by Esme's shrill, frightened scream from somewhere in front of the house. Leah dropped her cup to the ground and was running before she even thought about it, Marjorie close behind. They rounded the side of the house to see Sir Horatio dragging a screaming Esme toward his carriage. There were several soldiers standing near him and the maid who'd been assigned to watch Esme was nowhere to be seen.

"Esme!" Leah shouted, running to her.

"Mama!" Esme screamed and tried to pull away from Horatio toward Leah. Before Leah could reach her she was grabbed roughly by one of the soldiers and shoved back. Her mother caught her before she fell.

"She's my daughter!" Leah cried. "What are you doing?"

"Esme?" Leah heard Kurt cry out and turned to see him charging through the front door, the maid who'd been watching Esme close behind. Kurt bellowed with rage as he saw Sir Horatio dragging the little girl and he didn't break stride as he tackled the older man to the ground. Horatio let go of her and she tried to run to Leah but was snatched up by the same soldier who'd grabbed Leah. She was screaming hysterically by now, and Leah was crying, trying to get to her, but another soldier blocked her path.

"Let go of me, damn it!" Leah heard Kurt shout, anger and desperation in his voice. She looked over and saw two soldiers hauling him off Horatio.

"What the hell is going on here?" Valentine's voice rang with authority.

Leah turned to him with relief. "Valentine! They won't give me Esme!"

"Release her at once," Valentine demanded, his face suffused with cold rage.

Horatio ignored him. "Find the boy," he ordered the soldier in front of Leah.

"What did you say?" The tone of Valentine's voice caused the soldiers holding Kurt to look at one another nervously.

"You have no rights here, Westridge," Sir Horatio informed him snidely. "I've a writ from Sir Appleton, the presiding Justice of the Peace in the duke's absence. It gives me custody of the children, and was approved by the Duchess. They are mine now."

"This is my property," Valentine ground out. "It is you who

have no authority here. Give me the writ, and after it has been validated, I will consider the situation."

"Do you think me a fool?" Sir Horatio spat out. "If I allow you to keep the children until the writ has been verified you will spirit them away. As for your authority here, that is why I brought the soldiers. They are here expressly to see that justice is served."

"Justice, to steal children from their mother?" Kurt's tone was as virulent as Sir Horatio's. "This is not justice, this is cruelty."

"Sir?" Bastian's voice came unsteadily from the doorway.

"You, boy," Sir Horatio ordered him. "Come here. You are to go with me."

"No, Bastian," Valentine told him quickly as he hesitatingly started down the steps.

The soldier holding Esme passed her off to another and turned to Valentine with a look of contempt. "If you interfere, Westridge, you or your lover," he spat the word out as if it were an insult, "I have the authority to arrest you, and I will do so with pleasure. Your kind has no business around children."

"You cannot take them!" Leah cried out. "Valentine! Valentine, tell them! Tell them they can't take the children!"

Valentine stepped forward menacingly and the soldier reached for his sword. "Give me a reason, Westridge," he snarled. "You disgust me, and I'd like nothing better than to end your sorry life right now."

"Captain," Sir Horatio said with great satisfaction as he watched Valentine go still, "fetch the boy and let us leave this place. We are here to protect the children. I do not believe, unless he attacks us, we have the authority to kill Mr. Westridge, or Mr. Schillig for that matter."

Leah stood helpless as Kurt cursed and raged and struggled, and Valentine stood still as stone as the children were led away to Horatio's carriage.

Before he climbed in Sir Horatio turned to Leah. "You know what you must do, Leah. I'll expect to hear from you shortly."

CHAPTER 11

"We must wait for Freddy," Valentine said again in a weary voice. For two days he had held Kurt back and listened to Leah's sobs. His heart was breaking at what was happening to them, to the children. The future had looked so bright, everything so perfect. He should have known it would all fall apart.

"We cannot wait anymore, Valentine!" Kurt argued. "Marleston is wrong, yes, in the head? If we do not get the children now, there is no telling what he will do to them. What he may already have done!" Kurt paced restlessly on the carpet, running his hand impatiently through his hair. He hadn't slept for two days, none of them had, and it was showing. His accent was heavy, his eyes wild.

Valentine sat forward and resting his elbows on his knees, he rubbed his face roughly. "If we attempt to take the children it may be seen as an illegal act that could outlaw us, Kurt. Considering the behavior of the soldiers it could even kill us. Where would Leah and the children be then? For now Marleston is forced to play the rescuer. He can do nothing to the children or it will weaken his claim. So we wait."

"How do you know the duke will come?" Leah's voice was raspy and weak from her tears and exhaustion. "What if he doesn't come?" She leaned against the door frame of the study, broken. She hugged herself as if she were cold. "I must give in. I must go to Sir Horatio and give him what he wants."

"No, Leah! You can't," Kurt told her in an anguished voice. "You can't, or you will never be free of him. Can you so easily turn your back on what we could have?"

"How can you ask me that?" Leah tone was just as anguished. "You show me a glimpse of heaven, and now I must return to hell. You ask me to choose between you and my children, Kurt, and I must choose Bastian and Esme." She covered her face with her hands and her shoulders shook with her sobs. Valentine rose to go to her, but Kurt beat him there.

"I'm sorry, my love, I'm sorry," Kurt whispered as he took her in his arms. Leah grabbed the back of his coat in tight fists as she burrowed into his chest, still crying. Valentine went to them both, he couldn't stay away. They were his life, his loves, his tomorrows. He gathered them both close in his embrace and they separated, Leah's head on his right shoulder, Kurt on his left.

"I will fix this," he whispered. "I will take care of it."

"Then do it." Marjorie Northcott's voice cracked through the quiet room. "He has stolen our children, and you sit here crying, waiting for some flighty duke. If he's that powerful, he will help us after we have the children back."

All three turned to look at her in astonishment. "Mama!" Leah cried. "Surely you don't blame Valentine!"

Marjorie shook her head sadly and closed her eyes in grief. "No, I blame the one responsible—Horatio." She opened her eyes. "He is evil, Leah. You know it. You know what he's done in the past. Even now he could be beating those children. Do you want them to suffer as you did? I did nothing to help you when you needed me most. I won't make that same mistake with Bastian and Esme. I won't let you make that mistake."

Kurt turned to Leah with a growl. "He hit you before the other night? Why did you not tell us this?"

Leah sat down wearily on the settee. "To what avail? What good would it have done to tell you my marriage was a nightmare? That while my husband was busy gambling away every cent we had, his brother stepped in and made my life a living hell? That he beat me? Can you change the past? I think not. It was enough that you offered me a future free of him."

"Leah—" Valentine began, his face distorted with rage, but Leah cut him off.

"Mother is right. I'm going to Sir Horatio. I will make him give me the children. I can't let him control my life anymore. I won't let him." She looked at Valentine and Kurt. "Take your rage and come with me. If you want to confront him, I won't stop you. But I won't wait with you anymore either." She stood and moved to the door.

Before she could reach it, both Valentine and Kurt intercepted her. Valentine took her in a fierce hug as Kurt stood beside them, vibrating with intent. "Yes, Leah, we will go. We will go now."

Valentine turned his head so that he spoke into her hair. "Yes, I have been a fool to wait for Freddy. If we must we will leave with the children. The world is quite large, and surely we will find our place in it. But my place right now is at your side, protecting our children."

He pulled away and Leah reached for both his and Kurt's hands. "Let us go and bring our children home then."

"Thank God," Marjorie whispered as she sank down on a chair, "thank God."

<hr />

*V*alentine and Kurt reined to a stop in front of Sir Horatio's house. They were alarmed to see servants carrying boxes and luggage out to waiting carriages.

84

"Here, is Sir Horatio at home?" Valentine called to one of the coachmen.

"Eh? Sure he's home, but he's leaving within the hour. Taking the poor mites to school he is, far away from their mama." The coachman shook his head as he spoke. "And who are you?"

"I am the children's father," Valentine told him as he dismounted. His voice was low and ragged, shaking with his rage.

"Thought 'e was dead," the coachman said suspiciously. "Their ma's getting ready to marry again."

"She is marrying me." Valentine's steps didn't slow as he answered the astonished coachman. The servants who moments before had been busy scurrying about were now quiet and watchful. More appeared as Kurt followed Valentine to the steps.

Suddenly the front door flew open and Sir Horatio appeared with the same Captain who had been at Cantley the day they took the children.

"What do you want, Westridge?" Sir Horatio demanded. "You are not welcome here."

"I want my children." Valentine had come to a stop at the bottom of the steps, Kurt on his right. His voice rang with malice and authority, and the stance of both men clearly showed they were familiar with violence and not afraid to use it.

Valentine saw that the Captain was armed with gun and sword, and he looked ready to take them down on the spot. Valentine was glad he'd insisted Leah stay home and let him and Kurt handle this. She didn't need to be involved in a bloody confrontation. If he and Kurt were killed, they would at least take Sir Horatio with them, and Leah would have the children back.

"Mr. Westridge! Mr. Schillig!" Bastian's voice rang from inside the house. They heard running and then a scuffle, and Bastian cried out. "Bugger it, let me go!"

Valentine could feel his rage radiating out from his body, turning the air thick with tension. Next to him, he felt rather than saw Kurt prepare to move on Sir Horatio and the Captain. After so many years fighting by each other's side he knew instinctively what Kurt would do. The Captain's battle experience showed as he too anticipated Kurt's move.

"Don't even think about it," the Captain snarled. "If you put one foot on these steps I have the authority to kill you, and I will do it."

"You are welcome to try," Kurt snapped back. "But it will not be I dining with the devil this eve."

Both men took a step forward, and Valentine's pulse sped up as he prepared to do whatever was necessary to rescue his children and protect Kurt. But further action was suspended by the rattle of carriage wheels and the pounding of horse's hooves nearing the house.

All four men looked to see a large ornate carriage pulling through the gates. Valentine felt the tension leave his body and breathed easier as Kurt stepped back to his side. From the corner of his eye he saw Sir Horatio put a hand on the Captain's arm and pull him back. Good, he knew who it was too.

Kurt stepped forward and opened the door of Freddy's carriage before the footman could do so.

"Kurt!" The duke's jovial voice came from within and a second later his red head poked out the door. He shared a delighted smile with all those assembled and descended from the carriage without a care in the world. His clothes as usual were the height of fashion and impeccably tailored to accentuate his tall, leanly muscled frame. *His shoulders are bigger*, Valentine thought, *and his eyes wiser. Freddy is growing up.*

A handsome man with curly auburn hair and a serious face looked out of the carriage, his stern gaze lighting briefly on each participant in the tableau before him. He went to step out of the carriage and Freddy turned back to him instantly.

"Do be careful, Brett. Watch your leg." Freddy reached a hand back to help him down the steps.

Brett Haversham frowned at Freddy and shook his head. "You

make me feel like an old woman, Freddy. Have I ever fallen out of the carriage before?" In spite of his words he took Freddy's hand and leaned on it as he jumped to the ground.

"No, but that's because I always lend you a hand." Freddy's reply was unrepentant and accompanied by his charming smile, yet there was a hint of tension in his voice. Valentine knew Brett could not stay mad for long when Freddy looked at him that way. He thought back to their conversation with Leah and for the first time wondered why Brett denied Freddy. Clearly he cared for him. Sir Horatio's voice brought him back to the present.

"Your Grace, how delightful to see you." The man's unctuous tones made Valentine's hackles rise.

"Yes, yes, of course it is," Freddy trilled. "Valentine! There you are. We come from London with Stephen at your urgent request, and arrive to find you gone! When we stopped at Cantley we were told we'd find you here." He walked over to Valentine and the two men shook hands like old friends.

"Freddy, it is good to see you. We missed you in London." He turned to the carriage. "Hello, Brett." He extended his hand and Brett limped over to shake it. He knew the other man hated when people made concessions to his injury. Freddy and Brett greeted Kurt while Valentine watched Sir Horatio seethe on the steps.

"Sir Horatio," Freddy addressed him, "what is this I hear about kidnapped children? Surely I have misunderstood." Valentine started at the thread of steel in Freddy's voice. When had he acquired that?

Sir Horatio was made of stern stuff, however, and stood his ground. "My niece and nephew are hardly kidnapped, Your Grace. They are here safe and sound with me, as I'm sure my brother would have wanted."

Ah so that's going to be his argument here, Valentine thought with satisfaction. It was weak and easily surmounted.

"Children should be with their mother, Freddy," Valentine

smoothly countered. "My fiancée Leah, the children's mother, is most distressed."

"I quite agree, Valentine, at least in this instance." Freddy turned once again to Sir Horatio. "Bring the children to me, Marleston. I shall question them."

For the first time Sir Horatio seemed uneasy. "Your Grace, it would unduly distress them, to be sure. Their mother has chosen a, shall we say, unfortunate future with these two gentlemen, and the children were only too glad to be taken away from such unnatural goings-on. Your mother—"

Freddy interrupted him with a frown. "My mother is no longer in the neighborhood. Upon hearing of my imminent arrival she very wisely took herself off to parts unknown. Produce the children."

For the first time the Captain spoke. "Sir Horatio speaks the truth, Your Grace. You are clearly unaware of the disgusting nature of the relationship between these two or you would not call them friends."

When Freddy turned to the Captain, Valentine took a step back at the regal fury in his gaze. "Do not presume to inform me of the private lives of my friends, Captain. If I desire your opinion I will address you. Until then you are to keep your mouth shut."

"Freddy," Brett said quietly. Freddy's head whipped around to him. "Do not start with me now, Brett." He turned away, dismissing the other man in a way Valentine had never seen before. He was dismayed. What was going on between them?

A mask of congeniality fell over Freddy's features, and he addressed someone over Valentine's shoulder. "Hullo. And who are you, poppet?"

Valentine and Kurt both spun around. "Esme!" Kurt cried, and fell to his knees, his arms outstretched. The little girl flew down the stairs toward him. The Captain moved to intervene, and Esme slammed to a stop, huddled against the stone railing.

"If you touch her, Captain, you will find yourself escorting the refuse of Newgate to Australia." Freddy's tone was colder than Valentine had ever heard, and he knew without a doubt that if he were ever addressed in that tone, he would not hesitate to do whatever Freddy asked. The change in the heretofore easygoing young duke was nothing short of amazing, and a little alarming. Kurt had risen to rush the Captain but was stayed by Brett's hand on his arm.

"Your Grace!" Sir Horatio blustered. "I have a writ of custody for the children, approved by your mother. Surely you do not rescind that?"

"I do indeed, Sir Horatio. You seem to have forgotten the same thing my mother frequently overlooks. I am duke here, not her." He looked down as Esme quickly scurried down the stairs past Valentine and Kurt to tug on his coat jacket. As he looked down Esme held up her arms in the age-old childish way that indicated she wished to be picked up. Freddy obliged, and she leaned in and kissed him on the cheek. "Hmm, you've a smart girl here, Valentine. She knows where the man of true worth is."

Valentine was so relieved he could hear his heart pounding, and suddenly he felt the perspiration running down his temple from nerves that had been taut with tension. He laughed shakily. "Yes, indeed, Freddy. A very smart girl, like her mama."

The light moment was interrupted by Sir Horatio's furious hiss. "Fine, take the girl, she is useless to me. But the boy stays. He is my heir, after all, and British law favors my custody."

"No!" Kurt burst out in anger. Valentine knew it had taken great self-control to keep quiet until now. "You have no claim to these children. They are ours. Leah does not want you, accept this. We will not allow you to abuse the children as you did her. For that alone I should kill you." Brett had stepped in front of him and was holding him back with both hands on his shoulders.

Valentine heard an indrawn breath from within the carriage and turned to see Leah leaning out. He was as surprised as he was angry. What was she doing here? He'd told her to stay home.

"Mama!" Esme cried, and dove out of Freddy's arms. Leah caught her as Freddy let go. "Esme, baby," Leah said, kissing her face and hugging her tightly.

"Ah, and so you see, gentlemen, they always return home to mother," Freddy said dryly. "A chap has no chance against dear mama."

Leah laughed weakly. "Many a maid has no chance against a mister's mama, Your Grace. She is always to be found wanting, and he is the one who runs home to her skirts."

Freddy made a face. "You have met my mother, haven't you?" he asked teasingly.

"Your Grace!" Sir Horatio's tone was clearly admonishing. "Your mother is a great woman, and you should not malign her in front of these people." "These people" was said in the same tone as one might say "these vermin", and Freddy tensed again.

"Do you dare to take me to task, sir?" Freddy thundered, and Valentine winced. He looked at Kurt and the other man's eyes were wide in astonishment. "You who have so much to answer for?"

"Mother?" Bastian rushed out the door, his appearance disheveled. An angry footman followed, his eye beginning to black, his wig askew. Bastian eluded him and bounded down the steps, only to be brought up short by Sir Horatio's hand on his arm. He dragged the boy back, holding his arm tightly so only his toes touched the step.

"Ow, you're hurting me!" he cried, and Valentine rushed up two steps before Sir Horatio's words stopped him cold.

"One more step and I shall throw the boy down the stairs. He will be maimed for life."

"No!" Leah cried, and Kurt growled behind him. "You are a madman!"

"It has all been decided," Sir Horatio told them, his voice low and angry. "The Duchess promised me Leah. She said it was my duty to protect her from her base nature, to punish the children until they learned right from wrong. She promised me." He turned eyes glowing with hatred to Leah. "She was right about you. I should have known. You were always a whore. I couldn't beat it out of you when you were married to Thomas. I tried so hard to train you, to make you worthy of me. Look how you have repaid me."

Leah sobbed, and Bastian kicked out at Sir Horatio. "You bastard!" the boy screamed, struggling. Sir Horatio looked at him with distaste and Valentine's heart stopped. He started running up the stairs just as Sir Horatio flung Bastian away. He wasn't close enough, damn it! As if in a slow-moving dream Valentine saw the Captain reach out and snag Bastian, hauling him back from danger. With a roaring in his ears everything went back to normal, and Valentine didn't break his stride as he rushed Sir Horatio on the steps.

"You're a bloody dead man," he growled, grabbing Sir Horatio by the lapels and throwing him against the stone wall on the side of the steps. He drew back his fist and punched the smaller man with all the rage he felt and he could hear bones crunch at the contact. Sir Horatio fell to the ground, but before Valentine could hit him again he was grabbed from behind. It took a moment for the voice to register.

"Valentine, stop," Freddy kept saying over and over. When he was calm, Freddy released him and gently turned him away from the fallen, broken man. "Bastian is fine, and Marleston will not touch him again. I shall see to it, all right? Go get your boy."

Valentine walked over to the frightened boy, still huddled against the Captain. Valentine looked at the Captain, who was as pale as a ghost, his eyes wide. "I'm sorry, sir, I didn't understand. I didn't see." Valentine could only nodded in acceptance, over-wrought. "Thank you," he whispered to the Captain, and knelt in front of Bastian. The boy threw himself in Valentine's arms sobbing and Valentine held him close.

"Valentine," Leah sobbed, and he looked down to see her and

Esme in Kurt's arms. He picked up Bastian and went to them, went to his family.

When Valentine and Kurt had loaded the children into the carriage, Freddy bent down and hauled Sir Horatio up. He roughly dragged him down the stairs and threw him to the ground.

"You will leave here, Marleston. You will leave Derbyshire altogether. I do not want to see or hear from you again. Do you understand?"

Sir Horatio spit the blood out of his mouth, the left side of his face beginning to swell. "You have no right to throw me off my land." His voice wavered, with fear or hatred Freddy wasn't sure, and didn't care.

Freddy's vision dimmed with rage. "I am the bloody Duke of Ashland, Marleston. I not only have the right, I have the power. I have more money than God, land and influence, and when I choose to use it I can do damn near anything I want." He crouched in front of the now frightened older man. "I could wipe you from the face of the earth right now if I so choose, and not a hand would be raised against me. Instead, I will have my agent call on you within the next day and make arrangements for you to sell your estate. I have quite a few friends who are looking for country homes. It will not be hard to find you a buyer. By the end of the month I want all trace of you gone from my domain. Do you understand?"

When Sir Horatio made no reply Freddy stood and then suddenly kicked him in the chest, knocking him all the way to the ground. Freddy placed his foot against his throat and applied just enough pressure to make it hard for Sir Horatio to breathe. "I asked if you understood. Answer me."

Hatred burning in his eyes, Sir Horatio nodded awkwardly, struggling to breathe. Freddy stepped away and the older man coughed.

"Good. Pack your things and leave a forwarding address with the footmen I am leaving here to assist you in your departure. I will have my agent call on you."

"Leave now?" Sir Horatio croaked. "I must take care of my affairs here first, oversee the packing of my belongings."

"Someone else will take care of those things," Freddy said airily, waving his hand carelessly and already moving toward the carriage. "I simply cannot allow you to stay and ruin the wedding. Brett, do take care of it." Freddy climbed into the carriage then leaned out to say to Brett, "We shall wait a few minutes, my dear, for you to clear this up. Then we're off to Ashton Park."

EPILOGUE

*V*alentine's head fell back against the carriage seat as Leah moved exquisitely above him, fucking his cock slowly, trying to find a rhythm. She moaned, and Valentine hissed as she bore down deeply, hilting his cock. Kurt was busy kissing her, and his hands were touching both her and Valentine anywhere he could reach.

They'd only just left their wedding luncheon at Ashton Park and she was still wearing her wedding dress. Freddy had insisted they be married at his ducal estate. Leah had been overwhelmed at first, but she had quickly formed a friendship with Freddy, and Brett had given her away at their wedding.

"Oh," Leah cried softly, pulling away from Kurt's mouth and grinding down on Valentine. "God, I've been going mad this past week with you two refusing to touch me. This feels so good."

"Freddy locked you up at Ashton Park. And I wanted to wait," Valentine gasped, "for our wedding night."

"Well, you made it to the wedding afternoon anyway," Kurt said wryly, his own voice rough with lust.

Valentine tried to laugh, but it came out a groan as Leah slid back up his cock. "Oh, sweet Christ, yes, Leah," he panted. "Fuck me just like that."

Leah licked her lips and then grabbed both her breasts in her hands, squeezing them roughly. It was Kurt's turn to groan, and he kissed her again before running his lips down her neck to the tops of her breasts.

"You've gotten rather good at that," Kurt noted, kissing her hands on her breasts.

"Oh I've been practicing." Leah's voice was slow, wicked honey dripping from her lips. "I decided the day after we first made love that for the rest of my life I would climax at least once a day." She looked slyly at him out of the corner of her eye. "With or without you." She closed her eyes as she pressed down hard on Valentine's cock. "Vive *le petite mort*."

Both men laughed, their voices strained with desire. "Absolutely. I quite agree," Kurt assured her. "But even if it's without our help, please let me know so I can at least watch."

Leah's laugh turned into a groan as Valentine's hips suddenly surged up hard and fast into her. She bit her lip and matched his rhythm, throwing her head back.

"That mouth," Kurt whispered, falling back on the seat beside Leah and Valentine. "I'm going to put it to good use sucking my cock as soon as we get home."

"Which," Valentine paused to catch his breath, "one?"

"Both," Kurt growled, and Leah came. Her cry filled the carriage, and Valentine slammed hard into her, pulling her hips tight against his. It was his turn to bite his lip, trying desperately to hang on to his control and not come as her tight, slick walls pulsed around him.

"That's one," he ground out as Leah began to collapse against him. He immediately pulled almost all the way out and then fucked hard and deep again, making Leah cry out and clutch his shoulders. "I'm not done fucking you yet."

"Thank God," Leah groaned and Kurt laughed.

Valentine grinned wickedly. "Consider it a wedding gift," he said. Then he turned to Kurt. "I've got one waiting at home for you too." Kurt leaned over and sank his mouth down on Valentine's. Valentine opened his lips and devoured Kurt's mouth, his passion making the kiss rough and wet.

Leah shivered in ecstasy. "Oh God."

Valentine pulled slowly away from Kurt, giving him one last nip on his bottom lip, and Kurt groaned. Then Valentine moved Leah up and down on his cock, his hands at her hips. "Remember what we originally told you, Leah? We want this with you, while we remain lovers."

"Do I get to watch?" Leah whispered, her voice trembling.

"That's the plan," Valentine told her, and this time when she came, he followed right behind her.

The End

Warning: The unauthorized reproduction or distribution of this copyrighted work is illegal. No part of this book may be scanned, uploaded or distributed via the Internet or any other means, electronic or print, without the publisher's permission. Criminal copyright infringement, including infringement without monetary gain, is investigated by the FBI and is punishable by up to 5 years in federal prison and a fine of $250,000. (http://www.f-bi.gov/ipr/).

This book is a work of fiction and any resemblance to persons, living or dead, or places, events or locales is purely coincidental. The characters are productions of the authors' imagination and used fictitiously.

ABOUT THE AUTHOR

Reviewers have called Samantha Kane "an absolute marvel to read" and "one of historical romance's most erotic and sensuous authors." Her books have been called "sinful," "sensuous," and "sizzling." She is published in several romance genres including historical, contemporary and science fiction. Her erotic Regency-set historical romances have won awards, including Best Historical from RWA's erotic romance chapter Passionate Ink, and the Historical CAPA (best book) award from The Romance Studio. She has a master's degree in American History, and taught high school social studies for ten years before becoming a full time writer. Samantha Kane lives in North Carolina with her husband and three children.

www.samanthakane.us
email@samanthakane.us

ALSO BY SAMANTHA KANE

Brothers in Arms

The Courage to Love

Love Under Siege

Love's Strategy

At Love's Command

Retreat From Love

Love in Exile

Love's Fortress

Prisoner of Love

Love's Surrender

Love Betrayed

Defeated by Love

Fight for Love

Valor

Daniel and Harry

Mercury Rising

Cherry Pie

Cherry Bomb

Cherry Pop

Birmingham Rebels

Broken Play

Calling the Play

Jacked Up

Misconduct

The Saint's Devils

The Devil's Thief

Tempting a Devil

Devil in My Arms

The 93rd Highlanders

Hamish

Conall

When Love Comes Calling (anthology)

Play It Again, Sam

Tomorrow

Islands

Made in the USA
Middletown, DE
27 September 2022

11350342R00064